DEVIANT

Karma Police Book Four

_____

SEAN PLATT
DAVID W. WRIGHT

STERLING & STONE

DEVIANT

Prologue

THIS TIME IT'S DIFFERENT.

I don't wake up in my new host's body so much as I'm hurled into it. The young girl sprints through a forest of shadows, branches whipping her skin as she runs for her life.

Flashlight beams bounce in the night behind us — people hunting for her.

A pack of dogs is panting and growling, huffing into the night.

The moon is barely a suggestion, giving me only enough light to see that the girl is wearing a hospital gown. She is barefoot, slick grass cold on her feet, rocks ripping into her skin.

"Help me."

It's a girl's voice, with a slight Russian accent.

I'm confused, looking around, thinking someone is with me. But I'm all alone.

Except I'm not.

"Help me," she repeats, this time in my head.

Who are you?

"My name is Irina Pochenko, and you're in my body."

This isn't the way it normally works.

I usually wake up in someone's body while they're passed out or sleeping, smoothly stepping in and taking over. When I leave, they regain control, unaware that I was ever there.

I've never popped in like this, while my host is still conscious, aware of my presence.

But Irina is now talking to me like I'm a hitchhiker.

I try to get a feel for details on my host, but everything is vague. All I can tell is that she's around twelve or so, and I'm not even sure of that.

What's happening? How did I get here?

"I don't have time to explain. I need you to help me escape them. I can't focus on their brains and control my body at the same time. I need you to take control."

Why me? Do I know you?

"You can swim, can't you, Ella?"

How do you know my name?

"They made me look for you after what happened."

What do you mean after what happened? You know me?

A gunshot punches the night.

"Here," she says.

And then I'm in control, stumbling at first as her feet hit the cold ground.

My instincts take over.

I roll to the ground, sliding down an icy river embankment, narrowly avoiding the rapidly moving water.

"I can't swim. You can, right?"

Yes.

"Jump in. This river leads to a waterfall. It's our only chance."

I dive into the water and am immediately freezing, down to my marrow. Water this cold is dangerous, but a hell of a lot safer than the people and dogs charging behind us.

We go under for a moment. I fight to get her head above water, gasping for air before going back under.

I feel Irina's panic.

I have to keep us alive. I don't know what she meant when she said that she's focusing on their brains, but I hope she's fast and can lose them because I'm not sure if I can help us escape them *and* their dogs.

I manage to get her head back above water before the current shoves us down the river, around a winding bend, and out of our pursuers' line of sight.

I can't see the waterfall, but the water's moving faster, and it's harder to keep my head above the surface.

I look at the riverbank — a lighter swath of sable against the inky black woods.

I'm not sure how far we've traveled, but it feels like we've put enough distance between us and our pursuers to safely exit on the other side, and find our way to wherever Irina is going.

But then I hear the barking. Too close.

I turn around just long enough to glimpse the lights following us along the riverbank.

Before I can formulate a plan, the current drags us back under.

In the rushing movement, something hits us, hard.

At first, I think we've been shot, but then as I feel movement scraping across Irina's back, I realize it's only one of the many branches trapped in the current.

We pop back up, Irina's long dark hair clinging to her face, getting in her mouth as we gasp for air, moving faster toward the crest of the waterfall.

Who are these people?

"The Hospital. But not a normal hospital. They do things to us."

What kinds of things?

"Terrible things."

I want to press for more, but her resistance to discuss what happened, or even think about it, is strong.

I wonder if this has something to do with Chelsea. Was her hospital part of some clandestine operation? And did it have anything to do with the Karma Police Jumpers?

We go under again, then back up in time to see the waterfall ahead. It's too dark to judge our height and determine if survival will even be possible.

Not that it matters.

We're moving too fast to escape our trajectory.

We approach the crest, and I can't help but panic. Somehow, I stay cogent enough to remember that I'll need to gulp some air before we plummet over the drop.

Then we're in free fall, hurled off a one-hundred-story building, plunging, surrounded by water as we race toward the waterfall's base.

The drop takes forever.

Untold tons of water pressure bears down on us, throwing us through a void and into the earth below.

I pray that the water isn't shallow and that there aren't rocks waiting to smash her body to pieces.

We hit the water.

We plunge.

Deep.

The force of the waterfall us pushes us deeper.

Lungs tight.

Need air.

A new fear now — we won't be able to surface for air quickly enough.

I kick with Irina's legs, pushing us away from the

torrent, desperate to reach the surface, now violently craving oxygen.

I can't tell which way is up.

The water is pitch black.

I am disoriented, getting dragged farther under the surface, yanked toward the riverbed.

Lungs are burning.

Irina wants to open her mouth, desperate to breathe.

No! We're almost there.

I push harder with my limbs, trying to slice through the water, yearning for the surface.

No, no, no, no.

It feels miles away.

Come on!

I can't hide my panic.

I've failed her.

We're going to—

We break the surface.

And gasp, sucking in deep mouthfuls of air.

"We did it! Thank you, Ella!"

Suddenly, darkness.

∽

What the hell happened?

Where is Irina?

Where am I?

I'm in a void, undiluted darkness in every direction.

I can't see anything.

I have no eyes, nor body.

I can't see — *or sense* — a thing.

And somehow, I'm here, nowhere, wondering what happened.

One second I was in Irina, and the next here.

Wherever *here* is.

～

"WAKE UP," says a man over a speaker.

I open my eyes.

I'm back in Irina. She's wearing a fresh medical gown, and is dry, though chilled in the cold room.

We're tied to a metal chair in a small, bare room. Blinding lights above us. Beyond the glass walls, I see shadows in the dark, people sitting behind a giant control panel. There are three of them, two men and a woman, I think, and I can barely register what seem to be lab coats.

The Hospital.

They caught us, but how?

How did we get back here?

No answer.

I can't sense Irina in her body. Is she checked out to wherever people go when I'm in them? Or is she here but unable to respond?

I haven't been in her long, but I feel a strong connection after surviving such a harrowing ordeal. Perhaps there's some other reason I feel a bond. Irina said she'd been watching me. Though I didn't know I was being watched, maybe some part of me was aware and felt it, making our connection all the more solid while I was in her body, no matter the brevity of our union.

To not have her here with me now makes me feel alone, and scared.

A square black metal pedestal, about a foot wide, slowly rises from the floor with a mechanical *whir*.

I feel a chill, not sure if it's some residual memory of Irina responding to the pedestal or something from my memories.

This place is oddly familiar.

Are these memories mine or Irina's?

Have I been here before?

Have I been tied to a chair like this, with people staring from behind menacing glass walls?

The pedestal stops its rise, standing about four feet tall. The top unfolds, like a box opening itself, to reveal a gleaming black globe, shiny enough that I can see Irina's terrified reflection staring into it.

What the hell is it?

The globe hums.

The pain is instant, sharp blades piercing my skull from every direction.

I start screaming, and cannot stop.

Chapter One

I WAKE to someone shaking me and yelling. "Come on, Darius! Get up!"

I open my eyes.

I immediately choke.

There's smoke everywhere.

Fire burning to my left and right, surrounded by long, tall rows of computer servers, most are on fire, an acrid, noxious, chemical stench worming its way into my throat.

I'm not sure where we are. Behind the walls of flame and smoke, it looks like a giant warehouse, filled with servers.

What happened?

Why are we here?

My head is throbbing. The world is askew as I sit up.

A twenty-something-year-old black woman is wearing a backward Mets cap, a black long-sleeved shirt, and jeans. She is kneeling down and trying to lift me up.

Janet.

Her name pops into my mind.

She's Darius's girlfriend. And she's terrified.

"What happened?" I ask.

She doesn't answer.

She's helping me stand.

My head throbs harder.

I reach back and feel a giant knot.

"What happened?" I pull my hand away. It's covered in blood.

"Come on, work with me!" She grabs my right hand, coaxing me to walk.

We stumble toward a doorway in the distance.

"What's going on?" I ask, coughing.

Her shirt is pulled up over her mouth. In a muffled voice she says, "You don't remember? They must'a hit your head real bad."

"Who?" I cover my mouth, trying not to inhale the thick black smoke.

She nods to our left, and I see two burning husks of what were once men, one still clutching a gun, for all the good it did him.

"Who did that?"

She shakes her head, pulling me through the thick smoke.

There's a crash behind us, twenty feet from the door.

We don't stop. Or look back.

Instead, we run.

We race outside the door and into a parking lot alongside the building: large, industrial, two stories.

I look for a car but see nothing.

The building is surrounded by barbed wire fence. The main gate is closed, with a manned guard booth. There are men in uniforms and rifles approaching. I'm not sure if they see us, or if they're rushing the building.

Sirens roar in the distance.

We've got to get out of here.

"Come on!" Janet points toward a gaping hole in the fence where it looks like the metal has melted away.

Lights bleach the night from above, the rapid thunking of chopper blades adding to the cacophony of trouble coming our way.

A man's voice booms from above: "Get down on the ground and put your hands behind your head."

"Run!" Janet yells, grabbing my arm.

I'm frozen in the spotlight, staring up at the chopper, wondering what the hell is going on.

"Why are they after us?" I ask, wondering if this has anything to do with Irina. Though it doesn't seem to, I'm sure that it somehow does.

"Come on!"

Gunfire erupts all around us.

They're shooting us?

I spin around, angry, searching to see our attackers.

A stream of security guards, or hell, a small para-military group in black gear, are storming toward us. I count at least six, two dozen yards away.

"On the ground!" one of them yells.

Janet grabs my arm again, urging me to run with her. "Come on!"

I don't know why, but my host's legs refuse to obey. I can't move. I'm not sure if it's fear, a miscommunication, or something else, *something worse*.

But I can't move, and they're about to catch me.

"Go!" I yell at Janet.

Her eyes are wide with terror. I can tell she doesn't want to leave me, but at the same time, she doesn't want to die. There's something bigger at play, some mission we're on that just went south in the worst of ways.

Someone needs to return to tell … *I don't know who.*

A name teases the tip of my tongue, but it's ephemeral,

gone before an associated memory can fill me in on any of this.

The only thing I know with certainty is that one of us needs to get back to tell our boss?

Our leader?

Janet runs toward the gaping hole in the fence. Just beyond sprawls dark woods as far as I can see. I'm not sure how far she'll get before the chopper finds her, but at least she's going to try.

More gunfire, from the men coming towards us, now trying to shoot Janet in the back.

I turn towards them, rage boiling inside me, eager to draw their attention, to put myself between Janet and their bullets.

I scream.

Three men in black, rifles in hand, raise their guns and turn them on me.

I raise my hands, not even sure why.

And then it happens — fire explodes from my palms, arcing towards the men and engulfing them in flames.

What the hell?

I hear another step behind me.

I try to turn, but I'm too late.

Something hits me, hard.

Chapter Two

I WAKE up to a screaming alarm.

I reach out in the darkness, find the phone, then grab and silence it.

I lay in the cozy bed, waiting for information on today's host.

But little is coming. Only a name, Brooke Sumner, age twenty-five. Then I see that she lives alone in an apartment in Anchor Harbor, Washington.

Everything is fuzzy beyond that.

I'm still trying to process what happened with Darius before he was knocked out, or killed, and to Irina before that. I feel like I'm back in that waterfall, plummeting towards something I can't quite make out — something that's waiting to hurt me.

I flash back on the fireballs streaking from Darius's hands.

Did that really happen?

It sure as hell seemed like it. Maybe Darius caused the fire and killed those men in the warehouse before getting knocked out the first time before I jumped into his body. Maybe that's why those men were after him.

I wish I had been in him long enough to make sense of what was happening, so I could learn more about both Darius and his enemies. Or maybe figure out his connection, if any, to my situation or Chelsea's kidnapping.

There seem to be two kinds of people I Jump into: random people who have nothing to do with me, and those who are connected in some way to the *Mystery of Me*.

These last two Jumps feel super connected. I'm not sure how Darius is linked, but Irina said that "they made me look for you after what happened."

Who are *they?* And what happened?

Are they Darius's group?

Did Irina pull me into her body, or was it some mysterious hidden hand, whether it be nature or a mystical force, that put me inside her?

If Irina is connected to me, then Darius must be too. He's a freaking man who can shoot fire out of his hands.

Pyrokinesis?

It doesn't make sense, but then again neither do body jumping assassins. This is a strange new world, and the more I learn, the more I realize I don't know anything.

I look at the phone again.

It's 7:04 AM and I need to get ready for work, even though I'm not sure what Brooke's job is. I only know that she leaves the house at promptly 7:45 each weekday morning.

I switch on the nightstand lamp and set the phone down, realizing that I've never seen one quite like it. I've used many phones during the last year or so jumping from body to body, and become proficient in all the various models and operating systems from cheap prepaids to one time when I jumped into a high-level Samsung employee and found myself with a prototype.

But this phone is something different.

I turn it over in my hand. It *looks* and *feels* like an iPhone, slim and glossy in my hand. It even has the fingerprint sensor. But it doesn't have the familiar Apple logo, a home screen, or a single icon from Apple *or* Android.

What OS is this?

I thumb through the icons, searching for any sign of an OS, but there's no information, and it's like nothing I've ever seen. Most of a phone's usual options are either locked away or missing — there's no app store or music program. Only the barest of bones.

I pull up the contacts and find a long list of people with official titles beside their names: Commander, Sergeant, Agent In Charge, Director, and Liaison. Most of these names are attached to a company: Advanced Dynamics.

Something about that name stirs a buzz inside me, but I can't find any concrete memories to make sense of.

I drop her phone on the nightstand then head to the shower.

Brooke's apartment is small but immaculate. Expensive-looking paintings grace the wall, mostly in neutral colors that match the blacks, grays, and whites in her place. Even her Ikea bookcases are eggshell, decorated with black and white knickknacks and book spines.

Brooke's closet is divided neatly in half. One side is business attire, conservative dresses — mostly black and gray — ivory jackets and creamy white blouses. The other side is split between workout clothes and what looks to be paramilitary gear — pants, shirts, gloves, boots, and bags of equipment. Nowhere in the closet do I see casual wear, or nice dresses for Brooke to wear out on the town.

What the hell do you do for a living, Miss Brooke?

I put on a skirt, a blouse, and a pair of black wedge shoes, check myself in the mirror, then grab Brooke's phone and head to the kitchen. There are a gun and holster draped over the chair, an ID card on the table.

Brooke Sumner. Lead Division Five Consultant, Advanced Dynamics.

A gun for a consultant job?

What is Division Five?

I strap on the gun, throw on a jacket, and head out the door, hoping that my host's brain will start filling me in on whatever the hell is happening here.

I grab a coffee and a bagel from a local coffee shop on the way to work, though I've no interest in either. But I never know with a host when their bodies will fail because I didn't properly feed them.

I take a few bites of the bagel on the ride to work, but I'm too anxious about whatever this Advanced Dynamics will turn out to be to enjoy a single one.

AD is twenty minutes from Brooke's apartment, tucked away in a business park filled with several low-rise buildings and a separate structure that's about twelve stories high, surrounded by acres of grasslands and forest.

The perimeter is also surrounded by a high electrified fence with barbed wire all along the top.

I drive up to the gate. There are four guards checking access cards, all wearing guns. There's also an oversized booth between the entrance and exit lanes with more men stationed, every one with a rifle at the ready.

What the hell is this place?

My stomach churns as I roll down my window and greet the guard with an artificial smile, certain that I'm going to come off as nervous as a terrorist trying to smuggle a bomb into a top secret location.

The guard is a good-looking young man with a buzz

cut. His eyes are deep blue and all business. His badge reads *G. Stevens*.

He takes my card, runs it through a scanner, hands it back to me, then waves me through.

"Have a good day, Miss Sumner."

I nod, roll up my window, then take the long and winding road toward the "business" park.

～

I PULL into a ten-story garage to the right of the main building. Cameras are everywhere. I've never seen so much security in a garage. There's quite a bit of distance between it and the building, but I'm met by an old man driving a twelve-passenger cart.

I get on. The only other person onboard, other than the driver, is a chubby man with thick black glasses and long dark hair.

The badge hanging around his neck from a lanyard reads *Stanley Jetker, Research and Development Engineer.*

Stanley is staring at me. I'm not sure if I know him. He's not triggering any memories, but so far today with this host very little has. It's as if her brain is on a *very* strict need-to-know basis with me.

I nod. "How's it going?"

"Good," he says, looking nervously down at his laptop bag.

Alright, apparently Stan is a bit of an introvert.

Uncomfortable, and not wanting to sit through a lengthy round of awkward glances and nods, I pull out my phone and start thumbing through emails as we drive from the parking lot to the main twelve-story building.

One of the most recent emails is from this morning at 5:20 AM, from my partner, Richard Wellner: *Attached are the files on Darius Williams, apprehended last night and sitting in containment awaiting interview. See you at 10:00.*

Darius!

These are the people that got him?

I swipe to download the file. It opens immediately, and I'm given facts about Darius that I hadn't learned in his body.

He's considered a Category C Threat, whatever that means, and is labeled a "Pyrokinetic."

Several parts of his bio are redacted, sharp black lines slicing through them.

What the hell is happening here?

I read the email again, focus on the word *interview.*

My host's brain finally feeds me information.

Apparently, I interview subjects for the Institute as part of my job. I work with Rich. Early forties, buzz cut like the guard, a drill sergeant's personality, without an ounce of cuddly warmth. He manhandles subjects before it's my turn to come in all smooth and reasonable.

Classic Good Cop/Bad Cop.

Brooke went to university to study behavior analysis, graduated at the top of her class, then landed a gig with the FBI, working as a liaison officer with both the FBI and CIA's long-thought-dormant Scientific Intelligence Division. While officially employed by the FBI, that was a loophole allowing Brooke to work for her real employer, the CIA, on American soil.

Now she spends her days working people like Darius — *Deviants,* according to the Institute. All supervised under the umbrella of Project Karma, a CIA black ops program much like the defunct MKULTRA.

Karma as in Karma Police, the assassin body jumpers I may or may not be one of? That can't be a coincidence.

I look again at the word *Deviants.*

This is what they call people with special talents like Darius. But how they get these abilities or how many people have them — Brooke's memories refuse to inform me.

I try to pull up memories of past interviewees but run straight into a thick wall of what feels like static.

Brooke's brain might be the most compartmentalized I've ever seen in a host. Details *should* be popping up as I access her memories, but I'm only getting thin snippets, the kind of pre-packaged lies you'd tell family and friends when you didn't, or couldn't, tell them that you worked for the CIA.

I'm not sure if these mental roadblocks are defense by design or just the way she's wired — like someone protecting themselves from trauma.

I think about the Deviant database and wonder if I'm in it.

Maybe *I'm* a Deviant, and body jumping is my ability.

We arrive at the main building. *Stan the Man* waves and wishes me a good morning, waiting for me to get off the cart before him.

And they say chivalry is dead.

I return the wave then head inside to whatever is waiting to change things forever.

CLAUSTROPHOBIA IS a burning blanket around me, closing in tighter as I descend into the bowels to Sublevel 3. I want to hit the button and go back up, get in Brooke's car, and race home. Red lights be damned.

Let her deal with this shit tomorrow. I want a sick day.

But I can't.

I'm in Brooke's body for a reason, and I can't just leave.

This might have something to do with Chelsea, and I'm not willing to abandon the girl. She was being held in a room somewhere with other people in comas.

What if that place is here?

It wouldn't surprise me.

The security only seems to get tighter as I make my through a winding labyrinth of identical hallways, cameras every few feet, with hand and eye sensors at key entrance points. I wonder how much access I have.

If Chelsea *is* here, can I gain entrance to her cell block?

I follow Brooke's memories through a security station where I'm told to place my hand on a reader, even though the guard knows me, before getting waved through a set of tall double doors.

Institutional hallways open to a lobby that looks like it belongs on Madison Avenue, instead of a … whatever the hell this is. Overstuffed couches line the long aquarium wall. The receptionist's desk is the size of a city bus. I pass with a friendly wave to Carol. She nods, barely glancing up from her monitor.

I pass her desk then head down a T-shaped hallway with six doors on either side, and past another set of doubles at the far end where an armed guard is stationed outside.

If I were to take a right, I'd be led to our offices. A left would take me to the cells where Deviants are held until we're finished processing them.

I look at the red double doors — the Interview Room.

I greet the guard, place my palm on a panel beside the doors, then wait until they click open.

I step inside.

The Interview Room is divided in half. There's a long table in front of a window, and another table on the other side, with a pair of chairs facing each other. A door on the room's far side leads to a back hall, where subjects can enter.

Rich Wellner is at the table sifting through files. He doesn't acknowledge my entrance. I get the feeling that his demeanor towards me isn't unusual. This man doesn't like working with me. I can feel it, though I have no associated memories to tell me why.

Did Brooke lock those away, too?

I take a seat and Rich wordlessly slides a file to my side.

I open it and see it's the same file I saw on my phone already, with more paperwork attached. There's precious little information about the place that Darius and Janet broke into last night: *DC1451*. I want to ask what the place is, but Brooke would probably know, so I keep my mouth shut.

I glance over the files while waiting for Rich to speak. Finally, he says, "Bastard took down four agents last night."

"Shit," I say.

"If it were up to me, he'd be dead already. But apparently, Howard thinks this freak can be turned into an asset."

I catch a look in his eyes that I can't quite decipher. He looks away.

"What do you think?" I ask, not knowing who Howard is or what assets Rich might be talking about.

"We'll see." Rich sighs.

A door opens and Darius is led to the table by an armed guard.

He's wearing gray coveralls, hands bound behind his back in a black metal casing. There's a matching metal collar around his neck, making the poor man look like a dog. He's bruised to shit, with stitches on his cheek and forehead.

Did they rough him up after they caught him, or was he injured already?

His eyes are hollow sockets.

He's shoved roughly in a seat at the table.

The guard leaves.

Darius stares at the table, not acknowledging the two-way mirror occupying most of the wall.

I look at Rich, glaring at Darius. Brooke's memories tell me that he does this to set the stage for the interrogation. Anxiety supposedly throws them off, thus giving Rich and Brooke an advantage.

I wait for Rich to look at me.

"You ready?" he asks.

I'm not sure what I'm supposed to be ready for. I have no idea what I'm supposed to do.

I hope it comes to me as I nod and follow Rich into the room.

Chapter Three

I STAND BACK in the corner while Rich goes to work on Darius.

He introduces us, then sets a manila folder in front of the prisoner, just out of reach — not that he could get it anyway, given that his hands are bound behind him.

Rich slowly circles the table. Then he stops. "You're in some deep shit, my friend."

Darius says nothing. Just sits there looking drugged or exhausted, staring at the folder.

"You killed four federal agents. You'll be lucky to get life in prison, probably in one of our black sites where we deal with you freaks. But it's even more likely that your luck has run out, and you'll get the death penalty. Are you ready to die, Darius?"

"I'm not saying shit," Darius says, looking up with a menacing glare. His voice so low it's almost a growl. "Where's my girlfriend?"

Rich meets his eyes, jaw clenched. "This isn't how it works, Darius. You don't get to ask *any* of your questions until after you answer *all* of mine. Do you understand?"

Darius says nothing. Doesn't even blink. Just stares down at the table.

Rich continues, "You were breaking into a classified data center. A data center that very few people even know exists."

I remember something in the documents about Site 1241 but didn't connect it to the data center. What kind of data center was this?

Rich takes a seat opposite Darius and folds his hands. "I want to know how you learned about this site."

Darius shrugs, his eyes still on the table.

Rich slams his fists down hard, causing both Darius and me to jump.

Darius's eyes widen like he's been slapped awake.

"How do you know about the data center?" Rich repeats.

Darius shrugs again, returning his seemingly affected sleepy gaze to the table.

Rich sighs and opens the folder, pretending to read it. But there's only blank paper inside. He's bluffing, staring at the empty sheet as if deep in thought.

He closes the folder and drops it on the table. "I don't think you're the type of guy who meant to get messed up in this, are you, Darius?"

Darius says nothing. His eyes are fixed on the folder as if he's afraid of what else might be in there.

Suddenly I hear Darius's voice, in my head.

"Oh, shit. This is so fucked up. Just gotta keep my mouth shut, wait for Ben to get a lawyer."

I'm staring wide-eyed, wondering how the hell I'm hearing Darius in my head. Then it hits me, why I'm here in this room. It's *why* Brooke works here, *why* she works with this sour old man who hates her kind.

Brooke is a Deviant, too. Or, in Rich's words, a *freak.*

24

Her gift is reading people's thoughts, and now, at least for the moment, that ability belongs to me.

Rich looks at me oddly, brow furrowed as if he's about to ask me something, though I've no idea what that might be. I feel like this interrogation is supposed to be played out in two parts, his and mine, and like the world's worst actor, I've forgotten my lines.

Brooke still isn't helping me out. Although maybe she is helping by picking up on Darius's thoughts.

Rich stands, then paces, looking at me expectantly.

I nod, hoping that's what he's waiting for.

It seems to be.

Rich repeats his question. "You aren't that kind of guy, are you, Darius?"

"No, sir."

"Then, please, let me hear your side. Tell me about the others, the ones who put you up to this."

Again, I hear Darius's thoughts.

"Just stay cool. Ben will take care of this. He's got to take care of this."

I step forward before I even realize what I'm doing, speaking before I've considered Brooke's words.

"Ben's not going to help you now."

His eyes widen, panicked like he knows I'm in his head.

I already regret opening my mouth.

I've spooked him. Now he'll be more cautious with his thoughts.

Rich, however, looks pleased. Like he was waiting to hear me confirm Ben's association. Though Darius is the one with blood on his hands, I can't help but feel that *Darius* is the victim here and that I just helped the enemy.

What the hell did I do?

Darius rocks back and forth in his chair, eyes distraught.

"I've gotta get out of here. Gotta get my hands free. Torch this whole fucking place until I find Janet!"

Rich is looking at me. He gestures, urging me to continue.

Reluctantly, I do. Maybe I can find a way to steer this toward a positive resolution for Darius. I don't know how, but I'm hoping that the answer will come to me quickly.

I sit opposite Darius.

He slowly looks up and meets my eyes.

For a moment, something borders recognition.

I pick up on his thoughts.

"Where do I know her from? She looks so familiar, but I can't place her."

I wonder if he can somehow see through this body, straight to the real me, the Jumper inside the host.

Or maybe he's run into Brooke before.

"Please, Darius," I say. "We're only trying to help you."

"Yeah, right. Ain't nobody ever tried to help me. They just want what I've got."

I look at Rich, but his face is blank as he watches from my spot in the corner.

I want to help Darius, maybe even get him a deal, but I don't know what I can offer and what's off limits.

I nod to Rich, then to the door.

He takes my lead and heads for the exit.

"We'll be right back." I stand, making sure to hold his eyes so he trusts me.

Darius nods.

I leave the room, shutting the door behind me and joining Rich on the other side of the mirrored wall.

"So, what's he hiding? Get anything? Did we get anything on The First Front or Niko?"

The First Front? What is that? And who the hell is Niko?

Obviously, I can't ask him any of these questions.

"Just Ben's name so far," I say, hoping like hell that that wasn't a piece of information I should've already known from the dossier.

Rich nods. "Well, it's confirmation that he's working with them. That they're behind this. Now we just need to find them."

I follow Rich back into the room.

Darius is looking at us. "Who the hell *are* you people? You're not cops, so why are you holding me?"

"No, we're not *cops*," Rich says. "We're CIA. But we *can* make this problem go away, or we can do the same to *you*."

His brow furrows. "What do you mean 'go away?' Y'all gonna kill me?"

"No, but we can send you somewhere less friendly, a place where you'll wish we *had* killed you. You don't want that, do you, Darius?"

He says nothing, his eyes back on the table.

"Listen, I know this isn't really you. You're not the terrorist type," Rich says, his voice calm and reassuring. "*Someone* put you up to it. Tell us where we can find them and we can work on securing your freedom."

Darius says nothing.

Rich nods. "You're loyal. I can respect that." He paces in front of Darius, "I used to have this uncle, Vito. He was, as you can probably guess from the name, Italian. I know I don't look it, what with the pale complexion and all, but I'm half Italian, on my mom's side.

"Anyway, Uncle Vito was an old school tough guy, pulled himself up by his bootstraps, hustled to make a business for himself, and all that jazz. But his son, Stevie, was a bit of a prick. He was thirteen, and I was seven. We were fighting over a Babe Ruth baseball card that our grandfather gave to me, Stevie thinking it should've gone to him because I was only seven. He was *big* into baseball. Like he lived and breathed it, had been collecting cards since *he* was seven.

"Vito walks in on Stevie kicking my ass, and he grabs Stevie by the back of his collar, smacks him right upside the face. Hard, too. And then he makes Stevie apologize. He also told him to hand over his entire card collection to me.

"I know, pretty fucking extreme, right? Stevie cries, whines, and begs his father not to make him give his cards away, but Vito won't relent. He tells him to do it and do it *right now.*

"So Stevie brings me his books and boxes full of cards, then hands them over while crying his eyes out. Then Vito tells us both something I'll never forget. He said, 'family is the most important thing in the world. The minute you let things come between you and your family, well, that's the minute you've turned your back on them.'"

Darius is staring at Rich, waiting for something that relates to him.

"I can understand that kind of loyalty. But this isn't that, Darius. Because look around. Your *family* isn't here. They weren't with you at the data center. They sent you and your girl to do a job *they* weren't willing to do themselves. You know what they call a guy like you, Darius? A patsy."

"I ain't a patsy," Darius growls.

His thoughts are back in my head.

"Gotta keep my mouth shut. Ben'll find a way to get us out of here. He won't let them hurt us. I know it."

Rich leans on the table, his palms flat on the surface, "What about Janet? Is she a patsy? Did they maybe use her to get you to do something?"

"She didn't have nothing to do with this. It's all me and me alone."

Rich pauses, then pulls a phone from his pocket and dials. "Bring her in."

Rich hangs up.

Darius stirs in his seat.

Her is obviously Janet. I wonder what Rich is planning to do. People are usually separated while being questioned. It's a great way to turn one against the other. But this isn't a routine investigation, and we're not regular law enforcement.

Moments later, Janet is ushered in by a guard, hands cuffed behind her back. Darius tries to stand, but there's a low buzz from the shock collar around his neck. He winces then collapses back into his seat.

"Baby!" she cries, trying to move toward him.

The guard grabs Janet's cuffed hands, reining her in.

"Thank you," Rich says.

The guard leaves and closes the door behind him.

Rich turns to Janet, then to Darius, a pleasant smile claiming his face.

"Good, we're finally all together. Maybe we can make some progress now. Please, would you care to take a seat?"

Rich leads Janet to the table, tells her to slowly sit down as he steadies her to make sure she doesn't fall.

"Everything's gonna be okay," Darius says, looking into his girlfriend's worried eyes.

Rich claps his hands once, "Ah, that's what I like to hear — optimism! And yes, you're right, everything *will* be okay. I only require a sliver of information which your boyfriend has rudely refused us so far."

Rich stands behind Janet and continues to talk. "I merely need to know where The First Front is hiding."

Janet shakes her head. "We don't *know* any First Front. This is all a big misunderstanding."

Rich steps closer to her and sets his hands on Janet's shoulders as if he's about to give her a massage.

She flinches.

Rich keeps his hands where they are, though he doesn't move to do anything — yet.

Darius's eyes narrow on Rich.

"So, let me get this straight, you just *accidentally* wander into a secure facility? *Accidentally* breach security measures and *accidentally* murder a bunch of people?" Rich laughs. "You two either have the world's worst luck, or you're the worst liars I've ever questioned."

"We want a lawyer," Janet says.

"You don't get a lawyer. That's not the way things work anymore. Not with terrorists."

Darius shouts, "We're *not* terrorists!"

"The law would say differently. Now, are you going to give me what I need or will Janet have to suffer?"

Rich's hands circle her neck.

She tries to squirm away, but he tightens his grip.

"Get your hands off her!"

"Tell me where they are!" Rich barks.

"We don't know!" Janet shouts again.

Rich slowly chokes her.

Darius shouts, "Stop it!"

Rich shakes his head, his gaze steely, still strangling his victim. "Tell me."

Janet gags, fighting for breath and struggling to stand, her face turning purple. Rich's hands keep her seated.

Should I intervene? He won't kill her, will he?

No, he won't.

He can't.

I stand my ground, staring helplessly, hoping Darius

will say something to stop this man. Surely Rich won't go all the way. Surely this is something they do, a routine they've worked out like Good Cop/Crazy Cop.

If I intervene, it'll screw Brooke big time.

And yet, if I do nothing, I might allow Rich to kill a woman in cold blood.

At first, Darius screams in my head, *"He's not gonna kill her. He's not gonna kill her. He's gotta be bluffing."* Then, *"Oh, my God, he is going to fucking kill her."*

"Fine, I'll tell you!"

Rich releases Janet's neck.

She gasps for air, her eyes tearing up, staring defiantly at Rich, and then at Darius, heavy defeat in both of their eyes.

Rich rests his hands on Janet's shoulders and says, "Go ahead."

"I don't know where they are. My main contact is an old dude named Kotke."

"*Kotke?* That a first or last name?"

"Hell, I dunno. That's how he introduced himself: *Kotke.*"

While Rich is acting like he doesn't know who Kotke is, a flash of something in his eyes says otherwise.

"And where did you meet?"

"Online. A support group for people with ... *problems.*"

"What kind of problems? Erectile dysfunction?"

"No. People with powers. The group helps us control them, gives us a place we can vent about the shit we go through. They help protect us from people like you."

Darius glares at Rich, one minor act of defiance, an attempt to retain some control. But inside, Darius knows that he's lost. He already gave Rich what he needed. And now he'll be at the man's mercy.

"What else?" Rich asks.

In for an inch, in for a mile.

Darius spills his guts. "We were sent to install a thumb drive."

"And what was on this thumb drive?"

"A virus, I think."

"You *think?*" Rich shakes his head. "And why would you want to install a virus in this data center?"

"I don't know. I swear. He just wanted it done."

"Kotke? You're sure about that?"

"Yeah, Kotke."

"Good. See, I told you this wouldn't be so bad." Rich smiles and pats Janet's back. "You two are *this* close to getting on my good side."

AFTER THE INTERROGATION, Rich thanks me for my assistance then heads to the Briefing Room where he can coordinate with other agents to find and capture Kotke. That should lead to the others. Judging from the conversation, Kotke once worked with AD, and it's a bit of a surprise that he's involved with The First Front.

I blow off a lunch invite from two other agents, telling them that I have a headache and that I'm going out to get some fresh air.

I spend my lunch hour walking around AD, letting Brooke's memories fill me in as I go.

The Institute has twelve levels above ground and another five below — that I know of. Brooke has clearance for only two levels, and judging from the amount of security in this place there's no way to breach security on the off chance that Chelsea's here.

Memories color the gaps, painting more of a picture of what's happening here.

AD is a front for the CIA Black Ops division working on top secret projects that most reasonable thinking people would associate with crackpot conspiracy theorists rather than the actual federal government. Most of it has to do with various components of psychic warfare using *Deviants*. They pick them up, interview them, and ...

The *and* is the question.

I head back to my office after lunch, close the door, search for info on the data center that Darius infiltrated with Janet, and come up empty.

I type in Chelsea's name and get a hit, a link to a file.

I click it, my heart racing.

I'm greeted with a message that reads:

INSUFFICIENT SECURITY CREDENTIALS
PLEASE ASK YOUR ADMIN FOR ACCESS

Um, no. Not going to do that.

So, she has a file. Does that mean Chelsea is here? Or at least *was*?

I click around until I find some names I do have access to — people that Brooke has questioned.

There's a case of a girl who could turn invisible for short periods of time. There's a file on a young man with nearly impenetrable skin. There's another one with a young woman with telekinesis. Many files have a category reading "GENERATION" with a number beside it: one through three, followed by a designation indicating either mother, father, maternal grandmother, maternal grandfather, paternal grandmother, paternal grandfather, alongside the relatives' names.

I wonder if this is how many generations of Deviants there are.

If there are generations of these powerful people, why hasn't the American public, beyond the conspiracy theorists, heard anything before now?

Maybe they have.

Maybe it's one of those things I can't remember from my old life.

But I don't think so.

Along with each case, there are links to audio and video files. I try clicking on a few, but I'm prompted for a username and password each time. Nothing comes to me — I'm sure this is beyond Brooke's security clearance.

Many files have large chunks of black text replaced with "[REDACTED.]"

There's also a line in each Deviant's profile which reads: SUGGESTED ACTION.

But the suggested action in each case is a letter designation, A through Z. None if it makes any sense to me. And I can't even click on the letters to learn more.

What are they doing with the Deviants after their interviews?

I wish I could probe deeper into Brooke's memories, but even the fragments feel like buried treasure. The more I learn, the more I want to know, and the more certain I am that I'm somehow involved in this program. Chelsea, too.

That has to be why I'm in Brooke's body. It's the only thing that makes sense.

I do a search for the assassin's words when describing the Jumpers: *Karma Police.*

But of course, nothing appears.

I search for the term "Jumper" and find a few files regarding suicides, but nothing supernatural.

I search "The First Front" and get several linked files, but none that open with my clearance.

Of course.

As I stare at the insufficient credentials message, a horrible feeling creeps over me.

What if someone is monitoring Brooke's computer? What if I'm looking up a bunch of files I'd have no reason to be investigating all at once?

Something else occurs to me as I stare at the insufficient credentials message: how much more I might be able to see with someone else's login info.

Someone higher up the food chain.

Rich!

Maybe I can pluck a username and password from his head. It's risky as hell, especially for Brooke. Her entire life could be ruined by my actions.

But for Chelsea, the chance is worth it.

I stand from my desk, leave my office, and walk quickly down the hall.

Rich's door is wide open, but he's not at his desk.

I go to it.

The computer is on, screen unlocked.

I quickly enter.

I type in Chelsea Caldwell.

Her file appears.

But then there's movement in the hall outside the door.

Shit!

I try to get something from the giant blocks of text on the page, but there's too much to digest in such short time.

I scroll down to SUGGESTED ACTION and see only K.

Is K Karma? Or ... kill?

Footsteps come closer.

Any moment, whoever is out there will pass by Rich's open door and see me.

I close the screen and rush from behind the desk.

I hit the open door and am met by Rich and two armed men. He looks at me, his eyes cold, and says, "What are you doing in here?"

Chapter Four

MY HEART RACES and I stare at Rich, trying to manufacture an answer to his question.

What *am I doing* in his office?

He's staring at me, waiting. So are the guards.

My stomach is rolling.

I want to vomit.

How much do they know?

Did someone get an alert that *Brooke* was searching for things she shouldn't be searching for? Did they see me on his computer? If so, there's no way out of this.

I can't believe I let my needs — to learn more about this place and see if Chelsea is here — come before my host's safety. I've always strived to act within the parameters of my host's life, and not engage in personal business, particularly the stupid shit that will get them in trouble, or damage their lives in any way.

They're staring at me, waiting for a response.

My God, how much time has passed?

How guilty do I look?

My mind screams RUN! But, assuming I somehow escaped this place and its many armed agents, what then?

The CIA, along with the FBI, has the resources to hunt a person down. Where can you possibly hide from people like this — an organization that probably has an entire division devoted to tracking Deviants?

"Um, I was looking for you," I say.

"What is it?"

"I had a flash," I say.

He says nothing. I continue.

"The First Front. I had a flash from Darius, and it didn't make sense at first. But I keep going back to it."

"What?" Now he's folding his arms across his chest.

"I saw a long, dark tunnel."

"A tunnel."

"Yeah, old transport or train tunnels."

I'm pulling this out of thin air, no idea if there are any old underground tunnels or caves around here.

"Anything else?"

I try to get a read on him, to determine if he believes me, or if he's waiting to interrogate me as to the *real* reason why I'm in his office.

"No, nothing else. But I thought that might help."

"Thanks. I'll pass it up the chain and see what they make of it. You ready for another interview?"

"Another interview? Who?"

"We got Kotke."

I swallow, hoping my anxiety isn't too obvious. "Yeah, sure, what do you need from me?"

"I want you to sit on the other side of the glass. Just watch and see if you can pick anything up. I'll get you if you're needed. Okay?"

"Yeah," I say, following Rich and the officers back to the interrogation room.

～

I watch, alone in the adjoining room as Rich waits for the officers to lead their suspect inside.

The door opens and they bring in a tall, thin man who looks late fifties. Long white hair hangs over his face. He's wearing black slacks, a bright blue dress shirt, and a loud yellow tie. His hands are cuffed behind him.

Something about this man feels familiar. I lean forward, trying to get a glimpse of his face, but he's refusing to look up. He probably knows someone is watching from the other side.

The officers set Kotke at the table then leave Rich with his prisoner.

Rich turns on a video recorder mounted on a tripod in the corner then looks at me, though I don't think he can see through the mirror.

"Mister Kotke, it's a pleasure to meet you. I've heard so much about you."

"Can't say I've heard about you," Kotke, grinning like a smart ass from behind his curtain of hair.

His *voice* is familiar, too.

Do I know him, or am I picking up on Brooke's memories?

I lean to my left, trying to look under his hair.

"I want my lawyer."

Rich explains that Kotke has no right to a lawyer because he's a suspected terrorist, more or less the same thing he already said to Darius.

"Of course. Use the Terrorism Card — hammer of the scared autocrat." Kotke smiles, practically begging Rich to take a swing.

"So, whose idea was it to infiltrate the data center?"

Kotke says, "I want a lawyer."

"I told you, you're not—"

"Then you may as well bring in your heavy hitter because I'm not saying anything else."

Kotke turns from Rich to the mirror, and I'd swear he's somehow looking right at me. Something clicks in the fog of my mind — a memory of me sitting in a room with a younger version of this man, by maybe a decade.

As quick as it came, it's gone.

My heart is racing.

I stare at him as if doing so will reveal more memories, allowing me to piece this mystery together.

A snippet of audio fills my mind, this man saying, "You're too much, Ella."

Ella!

He used my name.

I *do* know him!

I try to hold onto the bit of something, searching for a connecting memory, hoping to flesh it out, maybe get a visual memory to accompany the audial.

But whatever I have slips through my grasp, ephemeral, leaving me empty-handed like a child holding the lonely spool from an escaped kite.

Kotke lowers his head again, looking down at his folded hands.

Rich continues, "Where is he?"

Kotke doesn't respond.

"You don't want to be on the wrong side of history, do you?" Rich asks. "Tell us where Ben is. We just want to talk."

"*Talk*," Kotke says with a small laugh, then ignores Rich some more.

Rich looks my way. I still can't help but feel certain he sees me, even though he clearly can't. "Don't go anywhere."

He turns from Kotke and approaches my door. I hope I'm going in. Getting closer to Kotke will probably trigger some memories.

Rich steps through the threshold, closes the door behind him, then looks at me. "Well? Get anything?"

"No, not yet. Maybe if I go in the room with you both?"

Rich looks at me, his brow furrowed. I'm not sure if he's suspicious or mulling my offer.

His phone rings.

He fishes in his pocket and brings it to his ear. His face becomes pinched. He was hardly a relaxed-looking man to begin with, but now he looks downright anxious.

"Yes, sir," he says, then hangs up.

"What was that all about?" I ask.

"Director Fairchild wants to sit in."

A current of recognition purrs in my head. I'm anxious, wondering if I know Fairchild too. But that can't be it. Probably just Brooke's memories of her boss.

"Okay, so do you want me to join you or not?"

Rich looks at me like I'm an idiot to suggest such a thing. For a moment, I'm sure he's going to scold me, but he looks too distracted.

Condescending: "No. Stay put here and do your thing."

Rich heads back into the interview room and takes a seat opposite Kotke. Then he sits with his arms crossed, staring at the man.

Kotke lowers his head, hair concealing his eyes.

It's a standoff until the door opens behind Kotke.

A man steps through, early sixties or so, tall, good-looking in a corporate way, with short gray hair, piercing blue eyes, and a chiseled jaw. He's wearing an all-white suit that is clearly bespoke. And tucked in his pocket, a single red rose.

Another flash, this time, a name: Fairchild.

We're standing in a big room together. He's talking to me, though his words are missing from the memory.

Then, another one: the man sitting at a table with a little red-headed girl, both of them talking to me about something, wanting me to do *something*.

I feel like someone's punched me in the brain.

I'm staggering, trying to untangle the knot of memories.

Fairchild walks over to Kotke and in almost a whisper says, "Well, look what the cat dragged in. I should've known you were behind this. And if you're involved, then surely Ben is?"

Kotke doesn't look up, refusing to acknowledge Fairchild or answer his question.

Fairchild stares down at Kotke, his jaw twitching. He repeats himself, slightly louder. "After all this time you can't even say hi to an old friend?"

Kotke's back straightens violently as if someone grabbed him by his hair, yanked his head back and forced him to meet Fairchild's gaze.

"Stop!" Kotke yells.

"There we go." Fairchild's smile is thin as a sheet. "Tell me, where are they?"

Kotke's body starts to shake like his insides are on fire or being electrocuted, eyes darting around. He grunts through gritted teeth.

"S ... *stop!*"

Fairchild's fists are tightly balled, his knuckles white. He's a Deviant, too. And this is his ability, whatever *this* is.

"*After* you tell me where to find them," Fairchild says, still smiling.

"Okay, okay," Kotke says.

Fairchild's fists relax. He pauses his attack, waiting for Kotke to give up the location.

Kotke gasps, his eyes watering, glaring at Fairchild. He probably wishes his hands weren't tied, and that he could kill the old man. But he's at Fairchild's mercy, and defeat is already haunting his sunken eyes.

"Well?" Fairchild asks.

But Kotke isn't looking at him. He's looking through the mirror, at me.

I hear his voice in my head, *"Ella? Is that you?"*

I stare at the window.

How can he see me? How does he know *I'm* here? Not Brooke, but *me*, Ella?

I fall a step back, not even realizing that I've lost my balance until my back collides with the wall.

"Ella, is that you?"

I answer back, wondering if this telepathy works like it did with Chelsea.

Yes, it's me. Do we know each other?

"I knew it! Did Ben put you here to save me?"

I ... I don't know why I'm here. I can't remember anything.

"You don't remember anything? You don't remember me? What about Ben Shepherd?"

No, I don't remember you. Who is Ben Shepherd?

"Shit. You don't remember your own father?"

My father?

A scream bursts from both Kotke's mouth and his mind, right into my head. A shrill, painful siren. I feel Kotke's pain, like electricity burning my insides.

I stumble back.

Then the connection with Kotke is broken.

His scream leaves my brain, though I can still feel the agony as if my fingers were resting on exposed wire.

I look into the room and see Director Fairchild bearing down, and his eyes narrowed on Kotke's violently shaking body.

I need to do something. Stop whatever this is, Brooke's future with the organization be damned. Anyone that would participate in this, sitting by, complicit in torture, deserves whatever shit Fate throws her way.

I'm about to barge into the room when Fairchild turns from Kotke to me.

He can't possibly see me, yet there he is, staring.

His eyes widen. *"You!"*

Oh, God no.

I turn to run.

But my body locks up, fire rolling through me.

I fall to my knees, hard.

I try to resist, I want to stand, but my body, *Brooke's body*, refuses to obey.

I hear Fairchild in my head. *"Don't move or the pain will get worse, Ella."*

So he *does* know me.

Shit.

I say nothing, my body frozen.

His voice is back in my head. *"Such a shame that you chose to help them, though I guess I shouldn't be surprised."*

I don't respond.

I've got to get up.

And out of here.

I can't take the pain, nor escape it.

The door opens behind me. I turn to see him. But agony amps up from a six to a ten the second I do.

I freeze, head halfway turned as he circles me, eyeing me from temple to toe, a curious crease in his brow.

"So, this is what you do with my gift? Use it against me?"

Behind him, Rich is following, confused, looking at me on my knees in such obvious agony, the Director standing over me as though I'm guilty. "What's going on?"

"We've got an intruder."

"What are you talking about?"

"Brooke isn't Brooke. She's been hijacked."

"What?" Rich's jaw clenches. He reaches for his sidearm.

"It's Ella."

"*Ella?*" Rich says, his eyes wide like he sees a mythological creature.

A trio of officers enters the room behind Rich, hands on their guns as they await instructions. They're staring at me with the empty gaze of allegiance. These are men who will blindly follow orders. Men who can't possibly understand, or perhaps don't care, that I'm not the *bad guy* here.

Fairchild steps toward me. "Please, girl, stand up."

My body jerks up, obeying Fairchild's commands while still refusing mine. Fortunately, the pain has ceased, at least for now. But I can only move my eyes.

I'm paralyzed. Fairchild is eyeing me with a mix of anger and fear.

Why are they afraid of me?

The old man steps up, inches away from me, his eyes peering into mine as if trying to see through Brooke's stare to the *me* inside her.

He reaches up, finds my cheeks with his clammy hand, and roughly turns my head. I hate his touch, how he has complete and utter control of me, acting on a presumption of *ownership*.

I don't get to choose the bodies I inhabit, and I always do everything possible to respect the host. But I get the sense that this bastard *enjoys* controlling others.

"Welcome back, Ella. How *did* you get past our defenses?"

My jaw relaxes, him allowing me to talk.

"I d-don't know."

And I don't.

"What do you mean you 'don't know?'" Fairchild's calm teases aggression.

"I can't remember anything."

"Really? Nothing?"

"I can't remember anything before a year ago."

"A year ago?"

"Yes. Everything is blank before that."

"But you *do* recognize your name?"

I'm not sure how I should answer. Are these the Karma Police that the assassin is part of? If so, was she allowed to tell me what she did? Was she permitted to tell me my name, or that these people were looking for me?

Or did she break a rule by informing me? And probably another by shooting me rather than letting The Collectors claim my soul?

Are these The Collectors?

I'm afraid to say something that might bring harm to someone, whether that means Brooke or the assassin whose name I don't even know.

"It's the only thing I can remember. And it's still new to me."

Fairchild is still looking at me as if unsure of what to believe. He turns my face in his hands again, peering into my eyes as though I'm inhuman.

"Then what are you doing here?"

"I don't know. All I know is that I wake up in a different body almost every day. Then I try not to screw things up for the person I'm in."

He laughs. "So, how's that working for you today?"

I don't respond.

I look in the window behind Fairchild and the others, at Kotke sitting in the interrogation room, watching, wide-eyed. He looks like he's trying to tell me something, but I have a feeling that Fairchild is somehow stopping him from telepathic communication.

Fairchild catches me looking at him, turns to Kotke, then back at me.

"So, then it's a *coincidence* that on the night our data center gets hit, you just happen to wake up in one of our agents?"

I nod. "I don't know what's going on. I don't know who or what controls where I go. I feel like there's someone manipulating things, because the people I wake up in so often seem connected. But, as I said, I don't have any memories from before last year. None."

Fairchild nods. "*None?*"

"Damn it, I'm telling you the truth."

"Forgive me if I don't believe you, *Ella.*"

My name is bitter on his tongue. I wonder what happened between us? Did I betray him? Or this group?

"Why don't you believe me? What did I do to you? Who *are* you people?"

He turns to one of the guards and holds out his hand. "Give me your gun."

The guard unholsters his pistol and lays it in Fairchild's open palm.

"Bring Kotke in here," he tells the other guard.

What the hell is he doing?

I don't want to seem alarmed, lest he think I'm with Kotke. But my fear is hard to disguise.

The guard grabs Kotke by the hair, yanks him out of his chair, and guides him into the room where he stands before Fairchild like a scolded child.

Fairchild shakes his head, looking at Kotke. "Ever consider getting a haircut?"

"Fuck you," Kotke spits, kicking out, trying to get the old man in his knees.

Fairchild smiles while meeting my eyes. "You have us in an interesting position, Ella. We can't get to you in this body. And we're not going to harm our own agent, though I'm not sure that we'll ever be able to trust her again. She's more or less burned. So how do I get the truth out of *you*?"

"I *am* telling you the truth!"

"I don't think you are. And, if you didn't have this *convenient case* of selective amnesia, you'd know that I'm usually excellent at sniffing out lies. So, here's what we're going to do. You're going to tell me where your father and Niko are hiding. If that amnesia doesn't clear up, your old friend here will die."

"Don't tell them anything," Kotke says, not helping either of our causes. I told him that I couldn't remember anything, is he *trying* to get Fairchild to murder us both?

Fairchild turns. "Did I say you could talk?"

Kotke's mouth snaps shut involuntarily.

His face is shaking, sweat drenching his forehead, falling into his eyes as he struggles for control of his body.

Fairchild fishes a phone from his pocket, fidgets with something on-screen, then holds it up for me to see.

A timer, counting down from 57 seconds.

"Start talking."

"I told you, I don't remember anything. I wake up in a different body every day or so, and that's all I know. I swear."

Fairchild turns the phone so he can see it. "Forty-one seconds. Are you going to spend them all lying?"

"I'm *not* lying! How the hell do I get you to believe me?"

"You can't. The truth, and the truth alone, shall set you both free. Twenty-one seconds."

Fairchild presses the barrel of his gun against Kotke's head.

Kotke closes his eyes.

I hear his voice in my head: "Find your father. Find the catacombs."

The catacombs?

Fairchild looks at the phone. I can't tell if he intercepted Kotke's message or not.

The timer beeps.

Fairchild looks at me. "Well? Are you going to tell us?"

"Please, don't hurt him. If you think I'm lying, give me drugs or something to make me tell the truth. You can do that, can't you? Please, just don't—"

Fairchild pulls the trigger.

I scream as Kotke drops to the ground, his brains painting the wall to our left.

No, no, no!

You fuck!

"Why did you kill him?" I scream, trying to break free from Fairchild's grip. I'm desperate to step forward, to get in this monster's face.

My body is being dipped in fire.

The pain is too much.

There's no way to reach him.

But still, I *have to* try.

Pain is only temporary. I'm moving my feet to get used to the agony.

I'm planning to grab the gun in my holster.

I wonder if I can raise it quickly enough to kill him?

Though even if I can, there's no way the others won't retaliate and fill Brooke with bullets.

She knew what she was getting into working for these people.

Fairchild has to pay.

He must be stopped.

I try to step forward, but I'm still frozen.

Fairchild looks up and meets my gaze. "What are you going to do, *Ella*?"

He raises his gun.

"You're not killing me. You're killing your own agent. Are you ready to do that?"

I smile.

I've got him, and he knows it.

But Fairchild pulls the trigger and proves me wrong.

Chapter Five

I WAKE up to a little girl giggling, and bright sunshine pouring through sheer white curtains inside a *very* pink bedroom.

"Wake up, lazy daddy."

My head is aching from a nasty hangover. The sun is loud, just like the girl. I want to pull the blankets over my head and go back to sleep.

A flash of memory tells me who I am and jolts me awake.

I'm in the body of Brooke's partner, Rich Wellner. Whoever, or *whatever*, is controlling my journey seems to have reason to keep me here in this world of black ops CIA. That could be good if it's moving me closer to Chelsea or the answers to my life's big mystery.

How did Fairchild and the others see through Brooke? How did they know me? How was I involved with either the CIA program or The First Front?

I get flashes of Rich's night after Fairchild's murder of Brooke.

He didn't go home after helping to dispose of the body,

which was as dead simple a task as bringing it to a sub-level incinerator. What does it say about this place that they can kill an innocent person — *an employee* — and then just haul her down to the incinerator like garbage?

It hadn't been easy for Rich. At first he needed to pretend that this was somehow necessary and part of the job. As tough as Rich was, murdering an innocent person was a step too far. And afterward, he needed time to process what happened before he could see his family.

He called his wife, told her that he had to work late, went to a bar at the edge of town and got plastered, then drove home, not even caring if he plowed into a tree.

He found himself standing over his six-year-old daughter, Emily, asleep in her princess bed, in her princess pajamas, in her princess room, living in this safe little bubble where most people were good, and evil was easy to avoid. A world where Daddy went to work at the CIA as one of the knights protecting the little princes and princesses of the kingdom from the dragons outside the castle.

But what if the monsters weren't outside? What if they were the very people "protecting" the kingdom? Rich wondered when the lines between good and bad, black and white, had grown so muddied.

And then he broke down crying.

Rich crawled into bed and lay beside his daughter, hugging her, wishing he could turn back the clock to when he *was* that good guy — before being compromised by a job that wasn't anything like he believed it to be.

Before he was part of a program hunting Deviants for "the greater good."

The hunt was designed to do two things: keep the world safe from the bad Deviants and provide a place for the good Deviants to live out their lives. The Agency even worked with a school to train the best Deviant kids they could find.

But under the surface, Rich knew that something was rotten. He figured as long as he didn't personally witness any of the worst things, he'd be fine with it. You don't ask the butcher how the meat gets made if you're grateful for dinner.

But now Fairchild has gone too far.

He's killed an FBI agent, Rich's partner, a young woman who'd done all the right things until *I* entered her body. Yeah, he considered her a pain in the ass, but what young person *wasn't* a pain in the ass to old bastards like Rich? He still liked her, and, if he were honest, he envied her wide-eyed innocence and idealism.

She didn't deserve what happened to her. Nor did she deserve to have her body burned to a crisp. She'll be a missing person case for a few days. Fairchild already ordered someone to work up a false narrative, how she'd been dating some sketchy men, and that one of them was getting too possessive.

The Agency will frame a man named Robert Harris for the crime — a bartender getting too close to some politicians for the CIA's comfort. Framing him for Brooke's murder, then having him "kill himself" once police close in on his location, will eliminate two pesky problems at once.

It won't matter that her body will never be found.

Or that Robert Harris's alleged motives will be tenable at best.

All that matters is The Agency narrative. *That's* the story that will be recorded as history, aired on late night news channels for years to come, with Brooke Sumner merely another victim of a lie. A bright light extinguished too soon.

The whole thing is rotten.

So Rich got plastered because if he didn't, he just might do something stupid — like grow a conscience and call a reporter. Or worse. But he couldn't afford to grow a conscience. Not with a family to protect.

If Rich did manage to find a reporter brave enough to run with the story (about as likely as a snowstorm in Haiti), it would paint a target on him and his family that they could never get out from under.

Even if they managed to find somewhere to hide, find a new job, and live under the radar, Rich would always be looking over his shoulder. Waiting for the day he'd walk into his house to find his wife and daughter dead, the gunman standing over their bodies, ready to tie up a final loose end.

Then it would be Rich painted with a false narrative — yet another man in America who killed his family before turning the gun on himself.

Emily's voice pulls me back to the present.

"Are you going to wake up, Daddy? It's almost time for our picnic."

My eyes adjust to an adorable little face with blonde pigtails, blinking as she smiles up at me. As much as I enjoy waking up alone in a body without any family to feign familiarity with, there's something about opening my eyes as the parent of a small child that always tugs at my heart. That look in their eyes, that unwavering, uncomplicated affection. There's nothing like it in the world.

It makes me wonder if I have kids out there in my Real Life that I know nothing about. And if so, do they think I abandoned them? Or that I'm dead? Is their father still in the picture? If not, who is raising them?

As lost as I've felt this year, I can't imagine the loss a small child must feel not knowing where their mother is. Or feeling that she's left them.

Tears are starting to swell. I'm not sure if *I'm* an emotional mess, or if it's the residue of Rich's feelings from last night. Probably both, not that it matters any more.

"Are you crying, Daddy?"

I wipe my tears. "No, honey. I'm just really tired."

I remember what Emily said about it being lunch time. I panic, realizing that I'm going to be late to work. How the hell can I let Richard go in, the day after Fairchild found *me* hiding in one of his agents? Surely, he'll be looking for my return. And if he finds me in Rich, I'll probably get another agent killed, thus leaving this poor little girl without her father. Given how Brooke's body was disposed of, I'd be abandoning my wife and daughter to lives of heartache and mystery surrounding my death.

But I can't just stay home. That will be even *more* suspicious.

They'd probably send agents to the house.

Groggy, I say, "I can't go to the picnic. I've gotta get to work."

"But it's Saturday. You said we could have a family picnic at the park!"

My eyes adjust to the light enough that I can now see the disappointment in Emily's big blue eyes.

She's right. It *is* Saturday, and Rich doesn't usually work on the weekends.

I sigh in relief.

Maybe I can get through the day without hurling another person into danger.

"You're right, honey." I kiss her on the cheek and stand. "Let me shower and get dressed. Then we'll do our picnic."

"Yay!" Emily exclaims, then scampers away.

I make my way to the master bedroom where

Richard's wife Lindsay is changing into jeans and a plum colored tee.

She's in her early forties, same as Rich, with short blonde hair, pleasant laugh lines around her wise eyes, and something else — a pain I can see immediately. An ache she hides behind her public smile, but never with Rich. She doesn't need to, seeing how blind he usually is.

She looks at me. "Out *working* late, eh?"

No point in lying to her. Lindsay saw me passed out on Emily's bed, still in my now wrinkled work clothes. Hell, I reek of booze, half the reason I want to take a shower and freshen up.

"It wasn't a good day." This seems like the type of thing Rich would say. I can tell he isn't usually overly communicative with his wife, particularly about work stuff.

"What happened?" she asks, clearly concerned.

"I can't talk about it." I peck her on the cheek, then head to the shower.

I can feel her pain as I walk away, but I can't be extra affectionate if that isn't something that Rich would ordinarily be. That would only make things worse tomorrow or the next day once I left his body and returned Rich to his distant self.

Lindsay might be wondering why he was so sweet and loving one day, then back to normal the next. And knowing the little I do, I imagine that she'll think it was something she did.

I need to maintain the status quo no matter how painful or wrong it might feel.

I'd love to tell Lindsay exactly what happened, but I'm sure that would violate my rule. Besides, my confession would surely put her in danger. As far as she knows, Rich works for the CIA. He's one of the Good Guys. She doesn't know that he's part of a black ops group that experiments on people. I'm pretty sure that until last night, even Rich was in the dark about just how black his job could be.

Sure, protecting everyday people means working in the grayer areas of the law, where the real battles are fought. And yes, you must *sometimes* ignore civil rights for people who are obviously a threat. Rich could live with those things. The Bad Guys don't follow a code of ethics, so why cuff yourself with archaic rules and gift your enemy with the upper hand?

But killing Brooke?

And knowing that the only thing The Agency was protecting now was themselves?

No.

Rich got blasted to forget his complicity, to blur his reflection, to deny that he was the sort of man he thought he was fighting.

It wasn't the first time he'd gotten drunk or driven in that condition. It also wasn't the first time that the line between good and bad had blurred. But Brooke's murder was the biggest transgression. It was the thing you can never come back from. Proof of the thing he'd long suspected — that he wasn't working for the Good Guys.

Hell, maybe there are no Good Guys.

I shower, feeling terrible for Rich, and guilty for judging him so harshly when his hands were throttling Janet.

Inside him, I can see through his life's lens. He's not some bully on a power trip. If anything, he hates bullies and wants to squash them. He views people like Darius and the other Deviants out there as threats in a looming invisible war between humanity and what might one day replace it.

More of his memories flood my mind as hot water

beats on my body. As if it could wash yesterday away, or bring Brooke back or fix my screw-ups. But it does help me think and dive deeper into Rich's memories.

Navigating memories is like fishing, except that you can't ever be sure of which bait will attract which fish.

I start by thinking of something that *should* trigger an associated memory. But most people have associations I can't predict. For instance, if I try to think of what a host's favorite breakfast might be, I might imagine pancakes to see if that conjures any related thoughts.

But then I'm jumping from memories of pancakes to syrup to a time my host had a lot of syrup on their pancakes as a child. That triggers some childhood memories and traumas, which branches off to even more unrelated recall, and then I'm several layers removed from the original trigger with no way to harness a single thought.

It's not like a DVD player I can slow down or navigate to the desired chapter. It's more like the Internet on speed, with a broken keyboard and mouse.

As I try steering Rich's memories toward the Karma Police and Jumpers, I wind up seeing cases of him tracking down other Deviants, people with horrible powers doing terrible things. *Freaks* as he sees them.

But I'm not getting anything useful. If he's familiar with Karma, I'm not seeing anything.

Has he cordoned off parts of his memories, like Brooke did? He's not a Deviant, so I'm not sure how he'd be able to unless it's something the average person could be trained to do. Or maybe they've given Rich some sort of pharmaceutical cocktail to assist his psychic defense.

I try my name, Ella, to see what that might bring up.

Nothing.

How can that be?

Judging from his wide-eyed expression yesterday, Rich

recognized my name when Fairchild told him I was inside Brooke. He might not have known me, but he knew *of* me. So why can't I find any associated memories?

I'm jarred out of my zone by Lindsay's voice. "You going to be in there all day? Your daughter is waiting."

Your daughter.

An interesting choice of words, triggering associated guilt trips that Lindsay is always laying at his feet because they spend so little time as a family.

Lindsay hasn't worked since Emily's birth and was a restaurant hostess before that. When she went home for the day, she left her work behind. She can't possibly understand a job where you never really quit working. Where you're always thinking about the horrors you're forced to face. Where you're always worried how something might pan out.

He has not helped matters by never sharing. So instead, resentment has built through the years.

I would love nothing more than to break down the wall between them, to tell Lindsay everything and heal their divide.

It's a blessing and a curse to observe people's lives so objectively. I can usually see the precise things people should say and do to resolve their relationship issues. Ninety-nine percent of the time it comes down to communication. But people get so hung up on ego and not wanting to open themselves to hurt that they build their walls higher and higher until a meeting in the middle is nearly impossible.

It would be so easy to help Rich by talking to Lindsay. By telling her what he really feels, and explain that it does bother him that he works so hard and that he feels trapped in a job that might be endangering them all.

But Rich doesn't know how to escape, especially not

while keeping anything resembling a normal life. He's seen too much. A normal life is no longer in the cards. Lindsay and Emily would almost be better off if he was—

Then I see it, plain as day, a reason for the self-destructive drinking and driving. Why Rich is so cold to his wife.

A part of him wants to find a way out of their lives, if only to protect them.

A dead CIA agent is better than a live one, at least for a family. A dead man was a hero, not subject to a living man's flaws and weaknesses. A dead man also kept his mouth shut, which kept his family safe.

I feel sick to my stomach at this realization, and my inability to do anything about it. Even if I could figure some way out for them, even if I found some explanation which wasn't quite the truth, but was good enough to make Lindsay feel acknowledged, it wouldn't even matter once Rich was back in his body.

I'm not sure which is worse. Being Rich, unable to see what he needs to do. Or being me, seeing what should be done, but being unable to do anything.

I hate feeling so hopeless.

I finish showering, get dressed, then meet Lindsay and Emily downstairs.

"Ready?" I ask.

"Yes!" Emily leaps up and grabs a big picnic basket that's too large for her little arms. I try to relieve her of it, but she wants to carry it.

I smile at her, then we head out the front door and pile into the minivan.

Emily is singing along with the car stereo while Lindsay thumbs messages to her sister on the phone. I'm still not sure why I'm in Rich's body, but for now, I'll enjoy the moment with his family — one of the hundreds of similar moments with other people's families I've been a part of this year.

I can't remember each moment as they glom together. My brain seems to forget most details of my hosts' lives, but a few stick out, usually ones with precocious kids. And a few that were struggling with heartbreaking problems: cancer, the death of a parent, or extreme poverty.

I didn't have answers for those people, either. I could only try to be there for them, even if I was only pretending to be the person they believed that I was.

We arrive at the park shortly after one. Emily helps her mom spread out the food and drinks on a red and white checkered blanket. They've made sandwiches and fruit salads. Emily boasts that she made the chocolate chip cookies all by herself, though I'm sure that means scooping batter from the Tollhouse wrapper. But she's proud, and the cookies are good.

After lunch, we put the food away and lay on the blanket, staring up at low-hanging clouds, bright white and fluffy against the blue sky above.

Emily points to a cloud that she swears looks like a two-headed donkey.

"A two-headed donkey?" I laugh.

"Yeah, like the one in that cartoon."

I'm not sure if she means a cartoon with a two-head donkey or a normal one, but I agree. "Okay, I guess."

"Now you find one."

I'm scouring the sky but not seeing any that haven't already been claimed. "I got nothing."

"Oh, come on, Daddy. I see at least twelve more."

"*Twelve?*" Lindsay asks, either impressed or not believing her daughter.

"At least."

Lindsay and I trade bemused glances.

Lindsay says, "Okay, show us."

Emily points out animals, people she knows, and inanimate objects. Most are a stretch, but who are we to rain on a kid's imagination?

We're laughing and having a great time. For a moment, I feel like maybe Rich will be alright after all. He has a loving wife and a terrific kid. Maybe he wasn't giving Lindsay enough credit by shielding her from the parts of his job that he felt were too dangerous. Sure, there's a high level of secrecy when you work in the CIA, but there were ways to share things, hinting at the truth, while still working through some of the job's many issues.

Maybe they can mend their—

My phone rings.

The tone tells me it's Director Fairchild.

I go to grab it from my pocket. Lindsay shoots me a look: *Really?*

At least Emily isn't guilt-tripping me yet. She's still naming clouds, now well past twelve.

"Hello?"

"Wellner, we need you to come in."

Of fucking course you do.

"Why, what's up?" I ask, treading carefully so as not to arouse suspicion.

"We'll tell you when you arrive, but it's all hands on deck. How soon can you get here?"

"I'm with my family on a picnic right now."

"But you're in town?"

I consider lying, but I'm certain that Wellner's phone is tracked by The Agency.

"Yes."

"Get here ASAP," he says, then hangs up.

I look at Lindsay and Emily, both of them staring back with an identically sad expression.

They know what's coming.

Lindsay stands and starts folding the blanket.

"I'm sorry," I say to them both.

Lindsay doesn't look at me. I can feel a defensiveness rising, Rich's emotions still stirring inside, a part of him that wants to argue, *Hey, I came, and we finished lunch. It's not my fault that I'm getting called in. These aren't exactly people you can say no to. Just ask Brooke.*

"Why do you have to go in?" Emily asks.

"I don't know. I guess it's something big. He said 'all hands on deck.'"

Emily looks like I murdered her goldfish. "So does that mean no ice cream?"

I look at Lindsay, gathering the basket and blanket, then turn back to my little girl and her wounded eyes. "We can still get ice cream. He can wait a few minutes longer."

That seems to make her happy.

I wish Lindsay were as easy.

Chapter Six

AFTER ICE CREAM, and twenty minutes of unsuccessfully trying to conjure a way out of going to work, I drive the family back home then swap the minivan for Rich's Audi, and head to the complex.

My stomach is full of butterflies as I get closer to AD and contemplate what might be in store.

What if they're calling everyone in only to root out the Jumper? What if they have some automated scanner that can detect me? Even if they don't, Fairchild already spotted me once, which means he probably can again. Maybe there's more like him. Hell, the assassin Jumper recognized me a few times, so obviously there's some way to see through the host to the person in the driver's seat.

What if all of the assassins are there, awaiting my arrival? What if the Collectors are waiting to claim my soul, to once and for all end this limbo? Then it's not just Rich's life in danger, but mine.

I'm not ready to die, especially considering that I don't even remember my life before now or who I might be leaving behind. You'd think it'd be easier to die with no known connections. But leaving life behind without knowing who you were or who you might be abandoning seems somehow even worse.

After getting waved through by the guard at the gate, I park in the garage. There are only a few cars, so I guess *all hands on deck* means key personnel only.

Or maybe I'm walking right into a trap.

I get out of the car and head toward the main building, my stomach a ball of coiled nerves, all raw below my racing heart.

I push my way through the front doors and am greeted by Fairchild, who is standing in that same ridiculous white suit, with four armed officers.

I look around the lobby for others, but it's only me, Fairchild, and four armed men.

My mind screams, *Get out!!*

"Hello, Director," I say, hoping he can't see through to me.

"Hello, Rich. I hope you don't mind, but I'm personally screening everyone following yesterday's intrusion."

"Sure." My heart pounds in my throat.

He holds out his hand and asks for my pistol.

Can he already tell?

I do my best not to pause, drawing my weapon from its holster and handing it over without hesitation. He gives it to one of the officers standing behind him.

"Okay, Rich, I want you to stand there, hands on your head."

Shit. They're going to cuff me and throw me in some hole with Collectors to devour my soul.

"Sure," I say, trying not to appear nervous. Hell, he doesn't even need to be psychic to sense my rapid pulse, the cold sweat dripping down my back, or the heat I can feel on my face.

He smiles and steps closer, now only inches away. When I was in Brooke's body, he was looking down on me. Now I'm in a body about three inches taller than him, so he's looking up, but his gaze is no less intimidating.

I can't shake the feeling that he's staring through the disguise, right at me.

I meet the man's eyes, resisting the urge for any nervous banter that might give me away. If he's got me, he's got me. No need to make it any easier on him.

Fairchild stares into my eyes for an uncomfortably long time.

I brace for the attack that's surely coming.

"Relax," he says, his eyes still locked onto mine. "You don't have anything to hide, *do you?*"

Shit. I don't know how to answer. Humor might be the best approach, but what if it gives me away?

I answer straight-faced, hopefully not displaying my raw fear. "No, sir."

"Good. I'd hate to lose another solid agent."

He hasn't told me to lower my hands, and I'm not sure what's happening. Is it taking him this long to read me, or is he playing games before siccing his guards on me?

He raises his hand fast and I flinch.

Shit!

He smiles, gently putting his hand on my arm. "It's okay. You can lower them."

I do, though it's impossible to relax.

If he saw me yesterday, why can't he see me now? And even if he can't, there's no way he missed that flinch. But maybe that isn't an abnormal reaction given that he shot my co-worker yesterday.

"So, did I pass your test? You're not gonna shoot me?"

"Yes, Rich, you pass. I hope you understand our need for precaution."

"Sure." I want to ask so many questions, but I need to be careful. I'm not sure everything that Rich knows about this operation, and the wrong words will reveal me as an imposter. "What's up? Why did you call us in? Where are the others?"

"Upstairs, getting started. Did you think we'd wait for you?"

"No, sir," I say. "What is this? A new development with The First Front?"

"You could say that. But I need to show you something before your debriefing."

Fairchild walks towards the elevators. I follow like a trained dog.

He doesn't say a word as we step in the elevator, nor as it descends. The silence is deafening inside this big box, its black metal walls, thick enough to withstand a bomb seemingly closing in on me.

I still can't shake the feeling that he knows I'm in here and that I'm being decisively led into a trap.

What can I do if I am? They've already taken my gun.

I covertly assess my surroundings, searching for an escape. There's a hatch above, but the elevator is tall, and I'd need to jump at least three feet to reach it. I'm not sure if Rich's body will provide that level of athleticism.

I look at Director Fairchild. He's a thin man, but he doesn't seem weak. Hard to tell under his suit. It's also difficult to see if he's packing heat beneath his jacket, which I could maybe grab and use to escape.

I probe Rich's memories to determine if Fairchild is right or left-handed so I can figure which side of the jacket his weapon might be holstered, but I'm not getting anything useful.

I'm hoping I still have some of the fighting skills I'd picked up from my stint in Vinnie's body. I assume that

Rich also has extensive combat training, though nothing comes to mind.

The elevator halts with a hollow THUMP, then the doors hiss open to a narrow room and another security checkpoint with a pair of double red doors and another four officers.

This is where he's bringing me to draw me out or feed me to the Collectors.

Fairchild exits the elevator.

I stay put, my mind racing with possible scenarios, all of them awful. Part of me wants to hit the *Close Door* button then head back up and run for my life.

But there's no way I'd escape. Someone would stop the box and trap me inside. Or they'd have an army waiting on the top floor to grab me.

Rich is dead either way.

Maybe *I'm* dead either way.

Fairchild looks back at me. "Forget something?"

He asks like he's toying with me, as if he knows exactly who I am and is leading me deeper and deeper into his trap.

"Just trying to remember the name of those dolls Emily likes so I can pick one up after I get out of here, to make up for leaving in the middle of our picnic."

I step off the elevator.

Fairchild frowns. He isn't a man who takes kindly to being reminded of your sacrifices. To people like him, the job is the most important thing, *period*. Or at least it should be to anyone "lucky" enough to work at AD.

"Well, I'm sure you'll think of something," he says.

I follow him to the security station, then we both place our palms on a panel before being permitted through the doors.

We step into a cavernous all-black room, with a giant

black metal column rising from the center, its top vanishing into the dark ceiling some forty feet above.

The column is part of a massive computer system which serves as the backbone of the entire facility. Dozens of coal-colored hoses run from the column into the back of a large coal colored metal chair sitting in the center of the room, holding a young redheaded girl in a dull blue jumpsuit.

Her eyes are closed, moving rapidly beneath the lids. Her hands are splayed, palms down, onto the arms of the chair — lit with touch screens that seem to be reading her twitching fingers.

More hoses lead from the sides of the chair into circular recesses in the floor.

Rich has only heard about this room. And the girl isn't ringing any bells.

Yes, it feels familiar. Like *I've* been here before.

And *she* feels familiar, like a ghost from a past life.

The doors whisper shut behind us as we walk deeper into the room.

Fairchild is silent, his footsteps echoing on the highly polished black floor.

I feel like he's testing me, trying to make me slip and reveal my true identity.

Finally, Fairchild speaks, his hands folded before him as he looks up at the computer. "It's something, isn't it?"

"Yes," I say, cautiously.

"You've never been here before, have you, Rich?"

"No," I say, hoping I'm right. "So, what brings us here today? Is this the urgent thing you needed us for?"

"No. No, it's not. And I do have a confession."

Oh, no. Here it comes.

"I sent the others home."

"Why?" I already know and am hoping I'm wrong.

"Because they weren't you, Ella."

I should know better than to hope.

There's no point in lying. He can obviously see things that most people can't.

"You don't remember this room, or even Eden?"

"I told you, I don't remember anything before a year ago."

He looks at me, head cocked. "So you've said."

"And you still don't believe me?"

"I'm not sure *what* to believe."

"So why bring me here? Are you going to kill another of your agents, even though they've done nothing to you?"

"I brought you here to see if we can't solve your problem."

"What problem?"

"Remembering."

"And how do you propose to do that?"

"Well, I got to thinking about wasted opportunities last night. I have this," he waves his hands at either the girl in the chair, Eden, or the massive computer, I'm not sure which, "and I didn't even think to use it."

"What is this?"

"You still haven't figured it out?"

"Obviously not."

He speaks louder, "Eden, eject Cylinder seven."

"Yes, Mr. Fairchild," the girl's mouth says, her eyes remaining closed.

There's a hiss from beside me as one of the circles attached to a hose fills with light. Then something slowly rises from the floor — a long glass cylindric chamber, revealing either a sleeping or comatose woman inside, bathed in a crimson glow, a mask over her eyes, body strapped in place by metal bands.

"Project Karma Police. Still no bells?"

I lie, shaking my head, staring at the young woman. She's in her twenties, with short brown hair and pale skin. She's wearing an institutional-looking shirt and pants, which appear blue, but it's hard to tell with the red tinted chamber. Her garb reminds me of a mental patient, or perhaps a prisoner.

"How odd that you can't remember the program that *you* and your father were so involved with."

I walk around the cylinder, put my hand to the metal. It's cold and smooth to the touch. A memory triggers, me stepping into one of the chambers, but it's gone before I can examine it further.

"Is she in a coma?"

"No. Merely sedated."

I look around at the hoses. More than two dozen leading to circular impressions in the ground, more cylinders imprisoning additional Jumpers. "How many are there?"

He doesn't answer.

I wonder if Chelsea is only inches below in one of these cylinders. If so, how can I find — and rescue —her?

I try a different question. "Who are they?"

"Pilots and co-pilots, working together for a worthy cause."

"What cause?"

"Have you ever wondered why bad things happen to good people? Why a bomb goes off in a cafe killing dozens? Why a shooter enters a school and murders innocent teachers and students? Why terrorists fly planes into The Twin Towers? Why a pregnant mother driving to work is hit by a truck, killing both her and her unborn baby?"

"Because the world is a terrible place?"

"What if these things didn't *have* to happen? What if

we could stop them? Not all of them, but the ones that produce the most ripples?"

"Ripples?"

"Every event creates ripples which then affect other events, sometimes building towards something catastrophic. What if the bomb *didn't* go off in a cafe? Maybe one of the victims goes on to cure cancer. Or what if the planes didn't fly into the towers? Perhaps we wouldn't have gone to war, spending billions, losing so many lives, soldiers and civilians. Maybe half the Middle East wouldn't hate us, and we wouldn't have emboldened more groups to rise. Every action triggers another, and even the smallest ripple from a rock thrown into a pond can have a seismic impact. But what if we could catch that rock before it ever hits the water?"

He points to the girl in the chair.

"This is Eden, the world's first psychic Artificial Intelligence."

"She's not real?"

"Oh, she's quite real."

"I mean human."

He's quiet for a moment as if considering the question for the first time.

"She's a cyborg. You don't remember her?"

I shake my head.

"Eden can not only see trends and predictive patterns long before anybody, or anything, else, but she's not bound by our fears or limitations. Eden is helping to shape a better tomorrow. To finally make things right. Claim control of our fate rather than being at the mercy of chaos."

What he's saying seems impossible, yet I'm practically thrown off balance by an overwhelming sense of familiarity and truth. "What am *I* in all of this?"

"You were one of the first. One of the best."

"First what?"

"Jumpers. Psychics have been able to see the future for hundreds of years, maybe longer. But how can you control the game when you can't control the players? Enter Jumpers, people who can travel outside of their bodies and take over others. Paired with psychic co-pilot remote viewers, and Eden leading the entire thing, we're no longer powerless to change the future. We can target key people and mitigate the ripples."

"By killing people?"

"So you *do* remember?"

"I'm getting bits and pieces."

I don't remember anything new. I'm going on what I've already learned from the one assassin to help me, but I play along to keep him talking.

"It's not *just* about killing. Sometimes it's about *preventing* a death. Other times it's about being in the right place at the right time, being in the body of a politician about to cast an important vote, or in the shadowy rooms of the power brokers working to destabilize other countries. But mostly it's as simple as making sure someone doesn't miss a flight or preventing two people from meeting. You'd be surprised how little ripples turn into big waves. Each action we take is sowing the seeds for a better tomorrow."

"Wow, that sounds like an advertising slogan."

"The point is, *Ella*, we do *good* things. But sometimes you must do something *bad* to achieve something *good*."

"Like killing your own agents?"

Fairchild's smile fades. His brow furrows again. "That was an unfortunate event."

"And I take it your A.I. child didn't tell you that was going to happen?"

He stares at me, unamused by my sarcasm.

"So why are you telling me all these things now? You were interrogating me before. You killed your agent when I wouldn't talk. Now you're telling me everything. *Why?*"

"Because I believe that you really are lost, and can't remember. You'd be here with us if you could, helping Eden and our Jumpers."

"Helping you what, kill people?"

"No. To stop The First Front. To protect our kind from the coming war."

"What war?"

"A war between the past and the future. A war which The First Front are on the wrong side of. A war that you were helping us to win."

"Who are The First Front?"

"A group of Deviants who work to undermine us every step of the way. They don't believe in our cause."

"What do they believe in?"

"Chaos. Instability. They want to rise up and destroy humanity as it is. They poison Deviants against mankind. Their Jumpers are working actively against us, killing people we're trying to save, and saving those we're trying to kill. To put it simply, they're terrorists recruiting Deviants to their cause."

"Are they terrorists because they don't buy your agenda?"

"No, they're terrorists because they think humanity is expendable. Because they are working to create a world-wide extinction event to eliminate humans once and for all while allowing Deviants to survive."

Worldwide extinction event?

Those three words are a punch to the gut.

Fairchild's face is dead serious.

"How do you know you're right?"

"Because I see Eden's data. Because I've had the visions, same as our seers. We know what's coming if we don't act."

"So, what do you want from me? I told you I don't know anything, let alone where your enemies are hiding."

"Perhaps you don't. But you can find them."

"How?"

"Because you have a psychic connection to their leader."

"Who is that?"

"Your father, Ben Shepherd."

"My *father* is leading the people working against you? And you want me to bring you to him?"

"No, we want you to talk to him, to deliver a message."

"What message?"

"I'll give it to you later. First I need to know if you'll do it. Will you deliver the message, Ella?"

"I told you, I don't know how this Jumper thing works. I can't control who I Jump into. I figured it was random. It just *happens*. And I don't even know why I'm in anyone else's body at all. I assumed it was to help them, but nobody's ever offered instructions."

"We can guide you. The lack of control comes from you not working with us. Your father took you offline shortly before he left us. He didn't want you working in the program any longer. I believe he knew how instrumental you were to helping us. We didn't know his true intentions then, of course. It wasn't until after he left that we learned just how disturbed he was."

"How do you know all this?"

"You still don't remember me, do you?" Fairchild offers what might be his first genuine smile.

"No."

"I'm your grandfather. Your mother's father. I've known you since you were a baby."

His eyes and expression are honest.

I feel like another piece of my life's puzzle has just tumbled into place, even though I don't know what to do with it or how that new piece might fit into the bigger picture.

"You said my father pulled me out of the program, right? Then why am I still Jumping?"

"That, I don't know. I assumed that Benjamin had turned you, had you working with The First Front. But I should've known better. You're not like him."

So, the man who killed an innocent girl is calling me good? Not sure what to make of that.

"What is he like?"

"He was a good man once. But things started to go off the rails after your mother passed away. He bought into these conspiracy theories about the government killing Deviants, setting up death camps, and other nonsense. He fell in with some bad people at a vulnerable time."

It's weird. Here I am standing with someone giving me the first clues as to who I am, and yet I still feel so terribly lost. I have a million questions — each one more pressing than the others. I meet his eyes.

"You want my help?"

"Yes."

"How do I know you aren't just using me to find my father? You seemed insistent on getting his location from the other Deviants."

"Firstly, we *can't* follow you. That's not how Jumping works. You have a connection to him that will allow you to Jump into someone close to wherever he is. We can't follow unless we know that location. Secondly, we merely want to open a dialogue with him. Despite all the horrible things that The First Front has done, I don't think your father is evil. He just hasn't seen what we have. He doesn't know where his actions will lead us all. I believe we can come to some agreement — one that will enlighten him and our critics. One that can save the world."

"You'll understand if I find it hard to believe that you only want to *open a dialogue* given that I watched you shoot and kill two people in cold blood, one of them your own agent."

"Let me ask you something, Ella? Would you kill one person to save the world?"

I know the answer I'm supposed to say. But admitting it is difficult. My eyes go to the girl in the chair, Eden, still unconscious, communicating with the computer, or maybe the Jumpers or psychics in tubes beneath us.

Fairchild doesn't wait. "How about two people to save the world?"

Still, I say nothing.

"Do I feel bad about killing them? Yes. But not half as bad as I'd feel if I sat by and did nothing while events spiraled out of control. And that is what will happen if we can't talk to Benjamin soon — things will go terribly wrong."

"How do I know you won't kill my father if he doesn't listen?"

"You don't. And I can't make you do this. I won't kill you if you walk away, but I can show you more of our program, and you can understand why we do what we do."

"I'll help you on one condition."

His eyebrows arch. "And that would be?"

"I want you to free Chelsea Caldwell."

"Chelsea Caldwell? How do you know her?"

"I was in her body a month or so ago, right after she tried to kill herself. And I know you took her."

"Did you say *after she tried to kill herself?* While she was in high school?"

"Yes."

"And you said this was … *last month?*"

"Give or take a week, yeah."

Fairchild looks at me as if lost for words. He seems to struggle, then finally says, "What is today's date?"

I tell him.

"Come," he says, leading me back out of the black room with its computer and chambers stuffed with unconscious Jumpers.

I follow him back onto the elevator, and up one floor. Then down another corridor, this one all white, the floor shiny from a recent waxing.

We pass several closed doors, none with identifying names or numbers. Only lookalike black doors in large gray frames.

We follow the corridor until it ends in a T, then turn right, and arrive at a security station in front of a set of large double black doors.

We're waved through by the lone officer standing guard.

Beyond the doors, the place goes from clean, white, and sterile, to almost hotel-like, with warm browns, reds, and terra-cotta hues comprising the carpet's color scheme, walls, and doors, which now have names and numbers on the tags.

"What is this?" I ask.

"Living quarters for residents."

"In the Karma Police program?"

"Yes," he says as we stop in front of a door reading *11* and a brass plate reading *Pilot 71* on the outside.

He knocks.

Thirty seconds later a woman's voice says, "Hold on." Then ten seconds later the door opens, and I see Chelsea.

Except she's no longer the teen I remember. She's at least four, maybe five years older.

"Hello, Ms. Caldwell. I've brought someone to meet you."

She looks at me, eyes sparkling, smiling as if she's *happy* to be here. "Hi," she says looking up at me, then extending a hand.

If she knows it's me behind Rich Wellner's body, she isn't showing it, nor attempting any telepathic communication.

"Chelsea?"

She nods, "Yes. And you are?"

"It's me, Ella."

Her head tilts slightly, smile still on her face, now slightly askew.

"Ella … the Jumper who was in your body after you tried to kill yourself."

Her eyes widen. "Ella?"

She throws her arms open as if being reunited with a long-lost best friend. "Oh, my God, where have you been? I've been looking for you for so long."

"How long?" I ask, pulling out of the hug.

"Five years. Why?"

I feel Fairchild behind me, and want him gone. "Can we have some privacy?"

"Yes, of course." He nods then leaves us alone in the room, which looks a lot like any average hotel suite, save for a few books and art supplies that Chelsea's lined neatly on a small shelf.

I look at her. She's smiling. Is this Stockholm Syndrome, where she's been held so long that now she simply obeys?

"Are you okay? I thought you needed my help. You said some people in a van took you."

Chelsea laughs, but it sounds uncomfortable. I get the distinct feeling that she's being monitored and has to be careful with her words. "Ah, yeah. I *was* scared at first. But they've helped me to explore my gifts. They've given me a purpose here."

"What kind of purpose? Body jumping? Killing people?"

"I'm not a Jumper. I'm a co-pilot. I help Jumpers do their jobs, traveling with them psychically. Forget about me. Where have *you* been? I haven't heard from you or sensed you for five years. What happened?"

I tell Chelsea that until a few minutes ago, I thought I was still living in the year we'd met. "I don't know what happened. I can't remember anything for the past five years. Only bits and pieces of the year before I met you, and then a few fragments from after, but I don't know what happened."

"Come and sit," she says, leading me to her bed.

I take a seat beside her. Chelsea grabs my hand and tells me how much she missed me and that *really* everything is fine.

But as her mouth says these words, she's telepathically speaking others.

"You have to get out of here. Do not trust these people."

I knew it. How can I help you escape? You're the only reason I'm here.

"You can't escape. Forget about me. Just go."

"They want me to do something, to contact my father. I told them that I'd only do it if they released you. I can get you out of here."

She's maintaining her facade of a smile, but her eyes are getting wet.

"Please, just go. Don't do anything they say. They'll trap you here, too."

Her door hisses open, then another face from my past enters the room — Irina Pochenko, no longer the scrawny twelve-year-old girl running from The Hospital. She's now a beautiful seventeen-year-old young woman with long dark hair and bright gold and emerald eyes.

"Irina!" I stand to hug her, glad to see that she's okay, even if she's stuck in this place.

But Irina isn't smiling.

And I can feel Chelsea's terror behind me.

Irina speaks, sharply, "Is this how you repay our kindness? By conspiring behind our backs?"

Oh, God. Irina was listening in.

"I'm sorry," Chelsea begs, "please, don't tell them. *Please.*"

Two armed guards storm into the room and rush Chelsea.

I wish I had my gun. I'll have to improvise.

I turn to the closest guard and jab him in the Adam's Apple, causing him to collapse to the ground.

I go for his gun.

"Stop!" Irina screams.

My body is frozen as if she's paused time itself.

But I'm the only one affected.

The non-injured guard grabs Chelsea and drags her from the room screaming, "Please, don't hurt her!"

I want to yell, tell them to leave Chelsea here. To punish me, not her. But I'm still frozen, and I don't have to.

"Stop!" Irina yells. "Leave her here."

This isn't like when Fairchild had me paralyzed with pain. Irina has somehow severed my connection. I'm still in the host body, but can't access the controls.

I'm a helpless passenger.

I look at Irina, desperate to see whatever Rich is looking at. I wonder if he's back in control. If he is, I can't feel him in here with me, and he must be wondering what the hell is going on.

Irina walks closer to me. My vision follows, and I realize that Rich isn't in charge. *She* is, controlling everything.

Irina looks up at me. "So, I finally get to meet the infamous Ella."

I speak back in my mind, assuming she can hear me since she apparently eavesdropped on my conversation with Chelsea.

I thought you were good. I tried to save you from these people. What did they do to you?

"They showed me the light. A future where people like you and me aren't feared or maligned, a future where we make a difference. But there are so many of our kind out there giving Deviants a bad name. Who will ruin this for us."

She sounds like she's been brainwashed by Fairchild and Company.

Please. Let Chelsea go. Let her live a normal life.

"There is no normal for us, Ella. This is our birthright. Our duty."

Then I'm not helping you. I'm not giving a message to my father.

"Yes you will," she says, looking at Chelsea. "We might not be able to hurt you, but we *can* hurt Chelsea."

You won't hurt her. You need her, or she wouldn't be here.

My mind flashes back to Fairchild shooting Brooke Sumner dead in front of me. Irina shows me the memory.

"Need?"

Irina turns and heads toward the door.

For a moment, I think she'll leave me here, but then Rich's body follows, and there's nothing I can do to stop it.

We get back on the elevator and head back down to the black room with the girl in the chair and the Jump chambers.

Fairchild is waiting inside, hands crossed in front of him. "I had hoped you would do this willingly, Ella. But now you've forced our hand."

My body relaxes. My control has returned.

"Please. I'll do what you want. But please let Chelsea go. She doesn't belong here."

"I'm sorry, Ella. We've invested a lot of time and resources into Chelsea. She's a very special girl."

"She doesn't belong here," I repeat.

"And she doesn't belong out there. You saw her life before now. She was miserable. Her parents didn't understand her. She tried to kill herself. Now she's making a difference, doing good things in the world. And, until you arrived, she was happy."

"Bullshit."

Irina scowls at me. "Quiet!"

And my mouth shuts against my will.

Fairchild looks at Irina. "Let her talk."

Irina looks disappointed, as if she's upset her master, or maybe her father figure. What the hell happened since I last saw her?

"You want a preview?" She releases her hold, looks Chelsea up and down.

I look at Fairchild, who offers no denial.

"I thought you needed her. That she was *special*. But not so special that you won't hurt her to get me?"

"You're giving us a chance to end the war with The First Front before things get worse. I asked if you'd kill one person to save the world. You didn't answer, but here's mine: yes. *Every single time, yes.* No matter who it is. No one person is worth the fate of the world. *No one*."

"You people are *sick*."

Fairchild shakes his head, eyeing me with pity like I'm a confused child with no idea what I'm doing.

This only makes me angrier.

"I'm sorry you feel that way, Ella. In time, I hope you'll come around. Maybe when your father sees the light, you will too. Then we can all work together again, against our *true enemy*." He smiles at this thought. "Wouldn't that be nice?"

I say nothing.

"Okay, let's get this going, shall we?"

Fairchild commands Eden to eject two chambers from the floor.

They're side-by-side. As the glass doors hiss open, red lights illuminate the chamber interiors.

"Please," Fairchild says, waving a hand. "We don't want to make you."

I get inside one of the chambers, standing against a red cushion I'll be laying against.

I watch as Irina enters the other.

I glare at her as she climbs inside, wondering how someone could turn so thoroughly from good to evil.

I could feel Irina's kindness while inside her, when she was running from the overlords she worships now.

What did they do to turn her?

And are they doing the same to Chelsea?

I hate these monsters. I want to burst out of the chamber, find Darius's body, and use it to tear this place down.

I wonder how this is going to work, and why Irina is in the chamber beside me. Is she going to coach me, help me find my father? Fairchild had said that the Jumpers work in concert with psychics. Co-pilots. Is that what she is?

And how can they be sure that I'll stay here when I jump? I'm not actually in *my* body. I'm in a host. Does that matter? So many questions I should've asked instead of arguing the inevitable.

Metal bands close around my body.

No, not yet!

A sudden claustrophobic panic swells inside. I'm not sure if it's mine or Rich's. Shortness of breath, itches in places I can't reach, despite my desperate need.

I can't move.

I'm locked in place.

"No, please! Let me out for a second. I just need to scratch my back, stretch my arms."

The chamber door hisses shut.

"*No!*"

The chamber descends.

I would pound on the glass if I could move my arms, but I can't do a thing.

Something occurs to me as I'm lowered into the ground.

"Wait! You never gave me the message for my father! You never gave me the message!"

I hear a hissing all around me.

Then there's only the darkness.

Epilogue

I WAKE IN DARKNESS, gasping.

I sit up, catching my breath and wondering where I am.

The old digital clock on the cluttered nightstand beside my bed reads *5:15 AM* in bright red numerals.

My hand finds the lamp beside the clock, and I turn it on, illuminating a bedroom/workshop, stacked floor to ceiling with shelves, boxes, and crates overflowing with tools, supplies, scrap, and electronics.

The place reeks of metal, grease, and oil, all scents that Clifton loves, the odor of a satisfied life. Because nothing is better than being busy, having something to do, things to make, people to help.

How can he sleep here?

Details flood my mind.

I'm underground, in the body of Clifton Emmanuel, a 65-year-old man and one of the older members of The First Front. They call him The Fixer, a nickname he wears with pride. He isn't a Deviant with a super power or gift. He's just a *very* handy man, one who helped turned these forgotten catacombs under the city into a fully functional secret headquarters with power, running water, and all the amenities required to fight the government's black ops program.

There are others here, but I'm not sure how many, because one name is instantly at the top of my mind — my father, Ben Shepherd.

I get up, get dressed, and head out of the room into the winding labyrinth of stone passageways, following Clifton's instincts.

Nobody else is awake.

I turn down several hallways, descend a crumbling stairwell, the path illuminated by lights along the stone ceiling running every twenty feet or so between large swaths of darkness.

Finally, I find the gray metal door I've been looking for, in the concrete wall just like the others.

I knock three times, sharply.

The sound echoes off the wall.

A slot in the door opens, and I see a man's sad blue eyes looking back in the dim light beyond the door.

His voice is groggy. "What is it, Fixer?"

"I need to talk to you. It's urgent."

He opens the door and I see a man in his late forties, wearing a thick cotton jersey and jeans, hanging loose on his body. His dark hair, with strands of gray, runs just past his shoulders, curling at the ends. His eyes are faint blue, looking like they've been subjected to more than one life-time of sorrow. His beard is scruffy and his face gaunt.

And now that I'm staring at him, it's hard to believe I could have ever forgotten him.

Memories course through me, bits and pieces, but definitely memories of him, of us together.

"Dad."

"What?" he says, stepping back, confused.

"It's me, Ella. Oh, my God, I've finally found you."

My father backs up even further in his little room — less cluttered than Clifton's — and bumps into his bed.

He collapses on top of it, then sits straight up.

His eyes burrow into mine. "What are you talking about, Clifton?"

"It's me, Ella. I Jumped into Clifton's body. I'm back."

His hand reaches under his pillow.

And then his gun is on me.

He stands, eyes glaring, mouth twisted. "*Bullshit.*"

He puts the gun in my face.

Now *I'm* backing up.

Why doesn't he believe me? How can I convince him?

I put my hands in front of my face. "I swear, Dad. It's me. How can I convince you?"

I realize my error. I doubt I'd remember anything, even if he were to quiz me.

"You can't convince me. You're not Ella."

"Why is that?"

"Because I buried Ella years ago."

The story continues...

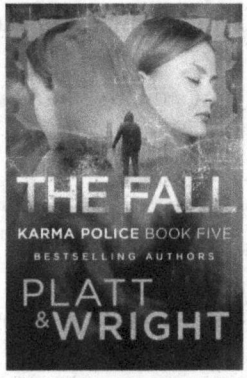

If you enjoyed reading *Deviant* and want to read more, the story continues in *The Fall*, Book Five in the *Karma Police* series.

Start reading The Fall today

A Quick Favor...

If you enjoyed this book, please take a moment to write a short review on your favorite online bookstore so other readers can enjoy it, too.

Thanks so much!

About the Authors

Sean Platt is an entrepreneur and founder of Sterling & Stone, where he makes stories with his partners, Johnny B. Truant, and David W. Wright, and a family of storytellers.

Sean is the bestselling author of over 10 million words' worth of books, including the Yesterday's Gone and Invasion series. Sean is also co-author of the indie publishing cornerstone, Write. Publish. Repeat. and co-host of the Story Studio Podcast.

Originally from Long Beach, California, Sean now lives in Austin, Texas with his wife and two children. He has more than his share of nose.

David W. Wright is the co-author of edge-of-your seat thrillers including the best-selling post-apocalyptic series *Yesterday's Gone*, the paranoid sci-fi *WhiteSpace* series, and the vigilante series, *No Justice*, as well as standalone thrillers *12*, and *Crash* which was recently optioned for a movie.

David is an accomplished, though intermittent, cartoonist who lives in [LOCATION REDACTED] with his wife and son [NAMES REDACTED.]

He is not at all paranoid.

He is "the grumpy one" on the *The Story Studio Podcast* with fellow Sterling and Stone founders, Sean Platt and Johnny B. Truant.

David writes about books, TV shows, movies, and

video games he enjoys; his struggles with anxiety and OCD; writing; and posts the occasional drawing at his personal blog at davidwwright.com

You can email him at david@sterlingandstone.net

We swear, he almost never bites. Unless you feed him after midnight.

For a full list of his most recent books visit sterlingandstone.net.

Also By Sean Platt

The Dead World Series

Dead Zero

Dead City

Dead Nation

Dead Planet

Empty Nest

The Beam Series

The Beam Season One

The Beam Season Two

The Beam Season Three

Robot Proletariat Series

En3my

Robot Proletariat

The Infinite Loop

The Hard Reset

Cascade Failure

Reboot

The Tomorrow Gene Series

Null Identity

The Tomorrow Gene

The Tomorrow Clone

The Eden Experiment

Karma Police Series

Jumper

Karma Police

The Collectors

Deviant

The Fall

Homecoming

Yesterday's Gone

October's Gone

Yesterday's Gone Season One

Yesterday's Gone Season Two

Yesterday's Gone Season Three

Yesterday's Gone Season Four

Yesterday's Gone Season Five

Yesterday's Gone Season Six

Tomorrow's Gone

Tomorrow's Gone Season One

Tomorrow's Gone Season Two

Tomorrow's Gone Season Three

Available Darkness

Darkness Itself

Available Darkness Book One

Available Darkness Book Two

Available Darkness Book Three

Also By David W. Wright

Cold Vengeance

Cold Vengeance

Cold Reckoning

Hidden Justice

Hidden Justice

Hidden Honor

Hidden Shame

Hidden Virtue

No Justice

No Justice

No Escape

No Hope

No Return

No Stopping

No Fear

Karma Police

Jumper

Karma Police

The Collectors

Deviant

The Fall

Homecoming

Yesterday's Gone

October's Gone

Yesterday's Gone Season One

Yesterday's Gone Season Two

Yesterday's Gone Season Three

Yesterday's Gone Season Four

Yesterday's Gone Season Five

Yesterday's Gone Season Six

Tomorrow's Gone

Tomorrow's Gone Season One

Tomorrow's Gone Season Two

Tomorrow's Gone Season Three

Available Darkness

Darkness Itself

Available Darkness Book One

Available Darkness Book Two

Available Darkness Book Three

WhiteSpace

WhiteSpace Season One

WhiteSpace Season Two

WhiteSpace Season Three

Stand Alone Novels

Crash

Emily's List

Threshold

The Secret Within